INVERSION IV

ANOTHER INFUSION OF SPECULATIVE FICTION

BY PAUL STANSBURY

First Edition
2022

Sheppard Press

Sheppard Press
461 Boone Trail
Danville, Kentucky 40422

Printed in the United States of America
ISBN 978-0-9986516-9-9 paperback
ISBN 979-8-9870989-0-5 e-book

Cover Graphics by Paul Stansbury

CONTENTS

INTRODUCTION

Inversion IV, Another Injection of Speculative Fiction, is my fourth volume of speculative fiction stories. If you are unfamiliar with my interpretation of what speculative fiction is, you will find the introduction to my first volume, Inversion, Not Your Ordinary Stories, in the Appendix.

As you might guess from the title of this volume, this collection contains more speculative fiction stories much like those in my previous three collections.

Inversion II and Inversion III each had a theme. The stories contained in this collection follow no theme which makes this closer to my first Inversion collection. So as the reader, you will find these stories taking place in a variety of settings. I hope this will suit your taste.

The majority of these stories have been previously published, either in print or online. I would like to express my appreciation to those editors who were willing to publish my work. I encourage you to visit their websites.

I would also like to thank the members of the Boyle County Writers Group, who have read most of the preliminary drafts of these stories and offered valuable feedback and assistance.

Finally, I would like to thank Joan Stansbury, affectionately known as the Queen of Commas, for her editorial assistance.

Paul Stansbury

MANGALO[1]

The days grew short and the nights welcomed frost. For so long, we waited while Mangalo slept. I in my lair, near him, beneath the cold dirt.

"So that's why you asked me to come over?" Danny asked. "There ain't enough leaves to make a good pile. Ain't even worth the trouble to get the rakes out."

Mangalo awakes with a gnawing hunger. He sends forth his thralls, compelling us with his foul mind. His hunger is our hunger. It is the time to hunt. I claw up through the dank earth. Above, the leaves are falling down. I hear every leaf touch the ground. As the wind blows them across the dying grass, they whisper that the time has come.

"There's enough," Tad shot back, "you're just too lazy. If there was a big ol' pile raked up, you'd be the first to jump in." "Ain't you afraid of the boogie man?" teased Danny. "They say he hides in the leaves and grabs you when you jump in."

"Maybe it's you that's afraid," snapped Tad.

"I ain't afraid!"

Mangalo's ravenous demands scream inside our heads. They fill me with such searing pain, I fear my skull would surely burst before I reach the prey. Unrelenting, the clamor pounds in my brain, driving me upward. None can resist the will of Mangalo.

"Come on then. It won't take long. Wait here and I'll get the rakes out of the shed," Tad ordered. "Just give me five minutes of raking and then if you don't think we have enough

---

[1] "Mangalo" appeared online in *The Weird and Whatnot*, 1/31/2019.

leaves, we'll quit and go inside to play some Minecraft. How about it?"

"Okay," grumbled Danny.

"Wait here," Tad said, hopping off the porch. He disappeared around the back of the house, reappearing a moment or two later, dragging two rakes.

The rocks and roots tear my scabrous flesh, black blood weeping from the wounds. Yet I crawl on, wriggling through the earth like a fish through water. The earth scraps over my body, closing tight behind, leaving no sign that I've been there. Driven on by Mangalo, I squeeze upward, the bitter dirt pushing through my lips coagulating with my spittle.

"Start over there," Tad said, handing one to Danny and pointing to the other side of the yard. "We'll meet in the middle."

The boys raked the colorful leaves toward the center of the yard, chasing the strays that the wind pushed away. Despite the fact that they would often stop to engage in a leaf throwing war, the mound of red, yellow, orange, pink, and magenta continued to grow until it was almost as tall as the boys themselves. It glowed in the afternoon sun, giving off a sweet scent which they breathed in.

The sounds draining through the soil grow louder, but not enough to overcome the call from Mangalo directing me toward his prey. I hear the footsteps of the children and the scratch of the rake's tines dragging leaves across the surface just above, guiding me to my destination. I hear their muffled laughter inviting me closer and closer. I smell the grass, the sweet decay of the leaves and the iron in their blood.

Below, Mangalo waits, impatient for his feast.

"See, that didn't take any time," said Tad, leaning on his rake.

"So, who gets to go first?" asked Danny.

"My idea. I get to go first. Anyway, you're too scared to go first."

"Oh no, I'm not," cried Danny, shoving Tad to the side. He ran toward the pile, leaping high into the air. He was already on the down arc when his feet hit the mound. The leaves offered little resistance as his body disappeared into the bright colors.

I crouch below the surface, the roots of the grass resting on my forehead. Mangalo's screams reach their crescendo. Still I wait. Wait for my prey's foot to touch the ground. Then I lung up, grabbing his legs. The earth snap shut above his head as I pull his writhing body down. Dirt spills into his mouth, smothering his screams.

Tad watched for a moment to see if Danny would jump up, throwing handfuls of leaves into the air.

Nothing.

"Danny, are you there?" Tad asked.

There was no sound or movement, save for a breeze rustling through the trees.

"Who's scared now?" Tad chortled.

Down, down I writhe, holding tight to my quarry. Down into the darkness until I reach Mangalo's lair. I lay the child before his gaping maw, the body still warm. Mangalo sucks sweet flesh from the bones, leaving the entrails for me. He belches, closing his eyes, and sleeps once again.

As Tad waited, a violent whorl of wind sucked the leaves up, leaving the ground bare where the pile had been. As the leaves drifted away, the harsh voice from below faded from Tad's brain. He smiled, knowing Mangalo would be happy.

NDOTO VUMBI[2]

James pulled the Elgin from his vest pocket. The watch read 7:39 p.m. It had been Colonel Winsted's during his long military career in Kenya. Upon returning to England, he brought James's mother along, installing her as his housekeeper. Djimon, as he was known then, was 8. He stayed with the Winsted family even after the Colonel's death, rising to the position of Butler.

James figured the nurse should be finishing bathing Will, who was Colonel Winsted's great grandson. James held his hand over the small pan on the stove. Satisfied the milk was hot enough, he poured it into a small working glass and placed it on the serving tray. It would cool to the right temperature for drinking by the time he made his way upstairs. He had already retrieved the small, worn ebony box he kept locked in the butler's pantry. In it, he kept his mother's special tinctures and powders. She had taught James how to make them and how to use them. He placed it on the tray next to the working glass.

James left the kitchen and climbed the stairs. He placed the tray on the nightstand, then turned back the bed clothes and plumped up the pillows while he waited for the nurse and Will to arrive. The familiar creak of the wheelchair announced their arrival. James met them at the door. "Thank you Sarah, you may go," he said, lifting the child from the wheelchair. He carried Will to the waiting bed. "I have some nice warm milk for you," he said, pulling the bed covers over the boy's lap. "There you are – the great giant of Counterpane."

"Yes, indeed," said Will.

"And did you dream of pirates last night?" James asked.

<hr>

[2] "Ndoto Vumbi" appeared online in *Down In The Dirt*, 3/1/2020.

"Oh, yes! Just as you said I would. There was a great battle between the pirates and the royal navy over Spanish gold."

"I trust the Senior Service won for King and Country."

"Quite!" Will's smiling face suddenly grew solemn.

"What is the matter?" asked James

"I heard the chambermaids talking. They said she was going to send me away to a 'sylum'. Is that true? I don't want to go away."

"Well, it must be that they do not have enough work to keep busy. I will set them to washing the windows. As for sending you away, I will have a word with the Lady. I am sure things will not come to that. Now, do not worry yourself with this anymore. Promise?"

"Yes."

"Well then, Master Will, what shall you dream about tonight?" asked James. "Perhaps flying in one of those new aeroplanes, or dashing about the countryside like Mister Toad in a stolen motorcar?"

"Oh, that would be great fun no doubt, but I should like to go to Kenya where you say you were born. It sounds like a grand place."

"Indeed it is, or so as I remember it, for I was but a young boy like you when I left. I am honored that you would wish to dream there. But, you can not start until you have had your milk."

"Did you bring it" asked Will.

"Yes, and the ndoto vumbi – the dream dust," James said, reaching for the ebony box. He opened the lid and selected three tiny vials from the many inside. He tapped a dash of powder from each into the milk, then handed the glass to Will. "Drink it up and soon you will be running with the lions. After that, you can climb

Mount Kilimanjaro. It will be good practice for when you are well enough to run through your own forest and climb your own trees."

Before Will put the glass to his lips, he wrinkled his brow and asked, "Won't the lions want to eat me?"

James smiled. "Not in this dream. The lions may be kings of the jungle, but you will be their Kaizari – their emperor."

Reassured, Will took a sip.

"Enough of this nonsense, James!" a harsh voice interrupted from the doorway. "I have rung for my tea. I should like for you to serve it." It was the Lady of the house, Mildred Fenkler.

"I was just tucking the boy in, Ma'am," said James.

"And filling his head with foolishness no doubt. It's time he learned to tuck himself in."

Will drained the last of his milk, then whispered, "Goodnight," before handing the empty glass to James.

"Sleep well, my little Kaizari," said James, taking the empty glass from Will's hand. The boy's eyelids had already begun to droop as James adjusted the bed clothes. He touched Will's forehead gently. "Ndoto gani unastahili - dream what you deserve."

James returned the vials to the ebony box, then picked up the tray and walked up one flight to Mrs. Fenkler's apartment. He placed the tray on a small table in the hall, then went inside.

Mrs. Fenkler was waiting in the anteroom, seated in a straight back chair. The tea service was already waiting on a small table inside the door. She glared as he looked about for the kettle. "It hasn't come yet," she said.

"Shall I go find the kitchen maid?" James asked.

"No, she will be here directly," said Mrs. Fenkler. "There is something I need to tell you."

"Yes Ma'am?"

"I have decided that William should go to the Blendon Sanatorium For Invalids."

"So it is true!" gasped James. "Surely there is no need for that. Master Will has all he needs here. Dr. Berdell says he is making progress and he has his nurse to insure his comfort. . ."

"And he has you to fill his head with nonsense," she hissed, "the false hope that he will walk again. And your obsession with dreams, filling his head with your heathen mischief. Dreams have no purpose other than to disrupt a night's sleep. Dreams will not make him walk again. The harsh reality is that he is bound to that wheelchair and that is where he will be for the rest of his short life."

"I do not believe that," said James. "I believe dreams can be powerful experiences. I believe some dreams can be so wonderful they have the capability to heal mind and body. I also believe they can be so terrifying the dreamer never awakens. I believe healing dreams will visit Master Will. I believe one day he will walk again."

"Pish posh," growled Mrs. Fenkler. "Dreams would not have saved my husband from the consumption and they certainly didn't kill him. Just as dreams didn't cause the train derailment that killed William's parents and crippled him. And it's obvious dreams didn't save them either. With regard to William's status, in the eyes of the law, he is an orphan. The fact of the matter is that I am Colonel Winsted's grandniece, whether you like it or not. As such, I am William's closest living relative, and therefore rightfully justified to assume the role of his guardian and sole trustee of his inheritance! As for what that means for the rest of you, don't forget all are here solely at my discretion. I will not abide insolence from the servants, whether it be a scullery maid or you!"

James took a deep breath, letting his anger subside. "No insolence is intended, Mrs. Fenkler. I simply request you reconsider your decision, as I believe Master William has a better chance to recover if he stays here."

"My mind is made up. He goes when the next bed opens up, which should be very soon. I trust this ends any further discussion of William and dreams."

Before James could answer, the kitchen maid appeared in the doorway. She held a tray with an ornate spirit kettle resting snugly in its stand. "Your kettle, Ma'am."

"I can see that, I'm not blind," barked Mrs. Fenkler, "Just set it down and you may leave. James will prepare the tea."

James carefully positioned himself so his back was toward Mrs. Fenkler. He poured some water into the waiting teapot. Next, he pried up the lid of the tea ball infuser and filled it almost to the top with crushed chamomile flowers. Then, he slipped his finger inside his collar and pulled free the gold chain which hung around his neck. A small black vial dangled from it. Bending forward, he pulled the stopper and emptied the pulverized mixture of thorns and desiccated spiders into the infuser. He snapped the lid shut and bobbed the infuser in the water until it turned a light amber color. Then he poured the concoction into a fine china cup. "Chamomile is an excellent choice before bed," he said, turning around with the teacup and saucer in hand. "It has a calming effect – good for the digestion and sleep, they say." He handed them to Mrs. Fenkler.

She inhaled the aroma then took a sip. "Very good," she said, "you are dismissed."

As he bowed, James whispered, "Ndoto gani unastahili."

9

"Did you say something?" Mrs. Fenkler asked, looking up from her cup.

James just smiled and turned away.

YOVIDO IN THE INVALDI SYSTEM[3]

The lander touched down with a slight bump. Wyatt sighed in relief. Although an extensive pre-landing analysis of Illio's moon, Yovido, had been performed, there were no guarantees when landing on an alien world.

"Me, too," said Macklin. He surveyed the rubble strewn landscape. "Can't see the crack," he said, referring to the narrow canyon that ran along the moon's equator. It was the only feature of interest on the ball of rock.

"Got eyes on it," Wyatt said, looking out his side of the lander. He tapped the touchscreen. Atmospheric readings popped into view. "Pre-landing readings confirmed," he said. "Nothing toxic. O^2 level at 93% Earth sea level. I've been reducing cabin O^2 by half a percent for two weeks. We should be good to go without oxygen assist. O^2 concentration should increase down inside the crack."

"Well, what are we waiting for?" asked Macklin. "Let's get our biohaz suits on and go picnicking."

"Not so fast. Gotta check environmental and biological readings first to make sure everything is safe."

"That's what we got the suits for," whined Macklin.

"Still, it's protocol," Wyatt said, examining the readings on the screen. "Gotta make sure we don't pick up any beasties that could cause problems later. I'm not seeing anything of consequence at this level. We're most likely to find something down in the crack."

"So, can we go now?"

* * *

[3] "Yovido In The Invaldi System" appeared in *Our Universes* - a Boyle County Public Library Chapbook published through Sheppard Press, 2019.

Macklin dropped the gear he was carrying a few feet from the edge of the crack. The terrain was too rough for the electro cart, so they had to carry everything by hand. He walked over to the edge.

"Be careful," growled Wyatt, placing his pack on the ground.

"Just want to take a peek," said Macklin. He peered into the chasm and sighed. "Guess I thought it was going to be something like the Grand Canyon. Not quite, but that sure looks like water down there. A beautiful blue ribbon running down its middle. "

"It runs almost all the way around this stone cue ball. Come on, we have two more loads to bring over before we can do any exploring."

* * *

Macklin touched the side of his hood to activate its built-in data screen. An hour had elapsed since touchdown. "If you wanted to bring everything in the lander," he complained, "we could have just dropped down here and worked right out of the storage bays."

"Too risky to try to hover this close to the edge," said Wyatt. He made a quick survey of the gear. "I think we've got everything we need. You want to send the drone over the side?"

"Well, yeah!" chirped Macklin. He flipped open one of the containers and retrieved the drone.

"Careful. We don't have a backup."

Macklin was too busy with the controller to acknowledge Wyatt's caution. The drone lifted off, floating a moment before dropping over the edge.

* * *

Wyatt and Macklin sat in the cramped lab cubicle they had erected. Wyatt was examining the samples brought up by the drone.

"The presence of liquid H_2O confirmed," said Wyatt.

"We knew that coming in, Sherlock. Tell me something I don't already know."

"There are trace amounts of a life form akin to Cyanobacteria much like our blue-green algae on earth. Oxygen producers, I would guess." He continued scanning the sample. "Wait a minute. There's something else here. Looks like it could be Yovido's version of siphonophores."

"What's that?" asked Macklin.

"Earth-type siphonophores belong to the phylum Cnidaria," replied Wyatt, "a marine species. Their distinguishing feature is cnidocytes, specialized cells that they use mainly for capturing prey."

"Whoa there, big fella. You're the biologist, I'm just the equipment tech. Plain English please."

"Jellyfish. Unfortunately, the suction tube on the probe was too small to bring up a specimen intact. Just bits and pieces here. We must get down there and bring back a live one."

"Is this jellyfish thing gonna put a damper on Wooten Outlands Exploration's plan to mine this rock out?" asked Macklin.

"Not up to me to make that decision," answered Wyatt, "but this, I would think, qualifies as a very significant find."

"Well, let's go get your jellyfish."

* * *

Macklin drove a piton into a narrow fissure at the edge of the crack and attached the rappelling line to it. "This rope is 230 feet. Should be enough to reach the bottom," he said, throwing it into the chasm.

"One of us needs to stay here," said Wyatt. "I'll go down and collect the sample. Once I get back, you can go down and explore some more." He hefted his pack. He leaned back over the canyon and gave the rope a final tug. Under the strain, the rock around the piton shattered. Wyatt teetered for a moment before falling backward into the void. Macklin rushed to the edge and watched helplessly as Wyatt careened off the jagged stone sides of the canyon and hit bottom.

Macklin grabbed the controller and sent the drone shooting over the side. As it approached, he kept his eyes glued to the remote display for any sign that Wyatt was alive. He was lying at the water's edge, motionless. Macklin guided the drone closer. On the screen, he could see Wyatt's hood had been ripped off and the side of his head was caved in. He was surely dead. A crimson plume billowed out, seeping into the blue-green water. Almost immediately, the water turned brown. Small creatures began to float to the surface. Even on the remote screen, he could tell their bodies were as lifeless as Wyatt's.

Macklin peered over the edge, watching in disbelief as the brown stain engulfed his beautiful blue ribbon. He realized Wyatt, so cautious about contamination, had never considered they would be the contagion that killed a planet.

UNNOTICED[4]

Martin walked down the long line of cubicles. The fragrance of lilacs told him Cynthia had brought in freshly cut flowers from her garden. Jack must have snuck out for a smoke, which was why a plume of aerosol air freshener was rising up from Elaine's nook. It held its own against residual cigarette smoke, but couldn't quite overcome Gina's knockoff designer perfume. Finally, he broke through to the ubiquitous aroma of tacos and breath mints that forever hung over Lloyd's burrow like the smog in LA.

"Hey, Marty. What's up?" asked Lloyd, looking up from the clutter of his desk.

"Not much. Gone to break yet?"

"Naw," Lloyd replied, tossing his pencil on a mound of papers.

"I'm headed that way," said Martin. "Diane'll meet us there."

"Come on," Lloyd said, standing up, "I'm tired of waitin' on ya."

They worked their way through the maze of cubicles into the hall, taking the elevator up to the 11th floor. The doors opened onto a corridor with restrooms on either side. Straight ahead was the door to the small breakroom. They entered the crowded room. It smelled of old banana peels and stale coffee. Martin saw Diane, sitting at a table on the outside wall, and gave her a nod before walking over to the drink machine and shoving a credit card into the pay slot. He punched the button for a bottle of spring water.

[4] "Unnoticed" appeared in *The Rabbit Hole, Weird Tales Volume 0* published by The Writers Co-op, 2020.

"Hey, get me one of them black cherry energy drinks while you're at it," Lloyd called out, pumping quarters into the chip machine. He studied the selections for some time before entering the item number on the touch pad. The corkscrew feed turned until a super grab of atomic pork rinds worked its way to the front and fell into the dispensing bin. Lloyd retrieved the bag, tore it open, and shoved a handful of pork rinds into his mouth.

"There's Diane," said Martin, pointing with Lloyd's pop can. "There weren't any black cherry energy drinks, so you'll have to settle for a lemon-lime."

"There were a bunch of them in there yesterday," said Lloyd. "Must be out."

"I didn't see a selection available for black cherry, only lemon-lime." said Martin. They zigzagged through the tables until they reached Diane.

"Hi," Martin said, sitting down. He caught a whiff of Diane's tea struggling past Lloyd's atomic pork rind breath. "What's the flavor of the day?"

"English breakfast tea with lemon," said Diane.

"Nice." He looked out the window at the brick façade of the building next door. "Some view."

"Well, at least it's a view," said Diane, taking a sip of tea. "Hi, Lloyd."

"There was yesterday," protested Lloyd, sitting down.

"Was what?" asked Diane.

"Black cherry," huffed Lloyd.

"What are you talking about?" asked Diane.

"Oh, he's miffed," said Martin, "because he thought the drink machine had black cherry energy drinks and he has to settle for a lemon-lime. Maybe they switched out stock last night."

"Why do that? I bought a black cherry just before I left yesterday," said Lloyd. "There were plenty left."

16

"Go see for yourself, if you don't believe me," said Martin.

"No, it makes sense," said Lloyd.

"What makes sense?" asked Martin.

"The black cherry disappearing. And the ghost pepper puffs are gone too."

"The what?" asked Diane.

"The ghost pepper puffs. They aren't in the vending machine, either." He took a long drink from his soda.

"I've never heard of ghost pepper puffs, much less seen them in our vending machine," said Diane.

"Well, there you go," said Lloyd, leaning over the table. He looked around to see if anyone was listening. "Just so you know," he whispered, "things are disappearing and no one is noticing."

Martin tried to hide his smile. "Lloyd, I think things disappear all the time and probably there are a lot of people who don't notice or even care."

"That's not what I am talking about."

"What then?"

"Marty, look at the top of that building," said Lloyd, pointing out the window.

"Okay."

"Can you see what's there?"

Martin craned his neck. "The fortieth floor?"

"No!" barked Lloyd, pounding his fist on the table. Martin grabbed his spring water to steady it. "Look closer," said Lloyd. "Notice anything on top?"

Martin studied the building. "I don't see anything."

"Precisely."

"Lloyd," said Martin. "There's never been anything up there. Right, Diane?"

"Sure," she said.

"There was a revolving nightclub up there two days ago," huffed Lloyd. "Don't you remember? The Top 'O The Town. Marty, we've knocked down more than a couple of beers up there."

"No way," Martin countered. "We've worked here a long time. I've looked out this window a thousand times or more. Don't you think I would remember a revolving bar on top of that building?" He looked at Diane. "Wouldn't you agree?"

She hesitated before saying, "I guess so."

"That's just the point," said Lloyd. "The Top 'O The Town was there one minute and gone the next. Listen, I was in here Tuesday morning getting *my black cherry energy drink and ghost pepper chips,* and saw the nightclub. But when I came back that afternoon, it was nowhere to be found."

"Maybe you need to layoff the energy drinks," said Martin, toasting Lloyd with his spring water. "And it wouldn't hurt to cut back on all those chemical-laden snacks. No telling what they dump in those love canal munchies. But, all that aside, I can tell you I don't ever remember there being anything, much less a nightclub, up there. Maybe you're remembering another building."

"It has nothing to do with energy drinks," Lloyd sneered. "Or snacks."

"Well," started Martin, "let's say for giggles that this nightclub was up there and it did disappear like you said. What happened? Did it fly off into space? I think not. Did they just demolish it and we didn't get the email? Maybe. Even so, wouldn't we have noticed the demolition crew? Wouldn't somebody have noticed? It's inconceivable, in this day and age, that no one would have taken a photo and posted it on social media. It would be big news, a news-at-six moment. How could such a thing happen and not be noticed?"

"I didn't say I could explain it," Lloyd shot back. "I just know it's happening. I know it sounds crazy, but I know what I've seen and no longer see. And I tell you things are disappearing."

"Hey man, you're the HR dude. Don't we have an employee assistance program or something like that? Maybe you should talk to someone there," suggested Martin.

"So you think I'm looney tunes?" asked Lloyd.

"Of course not," said Martin. He looked at Diane for assistance. "Diane, I didn't say that, did I?"

Diane looked down at her tea. "I don't know what to say."

"Just tell Lloyd I didn't say he was crazy."

"That's not it," said Diane. "I also think things may be disappearing. I've been afraid to say anything because I thought I was having hallucinations. But with what Lloyd said, maybe I'm just seeing things or not seeing things, as the case may be."

"What?" exclaimed Martin.

"It's true," said Diane. "It's been going on for some time now. At first it was just little things disappearing, like the receptacle in my cubicle where I plug in my space heater. Then I noticed the fire hydrant in front of my apartment building was gone. I tried to explain it away, just like you, Marty. I thought maybe maintenance had removed the receptacle and the fire department had relocated the fire plug, but when the old man in the park disappeared, I really got rattled."

"There ya go," piped up Lloyd, "case closed, the defense rests."

"Old men wander off all the time," scoffed Martin. "They usually find them wandering in their pajamas in the neighborhood where they grew up."

"No, he didn't wander off, he just vanished. In the evenings, I run in the park. I pass this older gentleman. Every day, he sits on the same park bench with his dog. He always smiles and waves when I pass by. About a week ago, I was running and could see him ahead sitting on his bench as usual. I took my eyes off of him for a moment to check my activity tracker. When I looked up, he was gone. The dog was there, but he wasn't."

"Maybe it was something like when you're driving," said Martin, "and you suddenly realize you've driven a couple of miles on autopilot without really noticing it. It's a weird feeling, but it happens to all of us at some point."

"There were lots of other people in the park," continued Diane. "No one seemed to notice. I checked the dog, no sign of his leash, no collar, but I would have sworn the old man always had him on a leash."

"Did you call the police?" asked Lloyd.

"No," said Diane. "What was I going to say to the police? Some old man vanished before my eyes and offer some dog without a leash or collar as my proof? It even sounds wacky to me. But I know it happened."

"Maybe it's some weird un-déjà vu," said Martin, "where instead of having the feeling you've already lived through something, you have the feeling that something has disappeared, when it wasn't really there to begin with."

"I don't think so," said Lloyd. "I've had déjà vu and it only lasts a few seconds, then you go on like nothing happened. These things that disappear are different."

"I agree," said Diane. "This is definitely not a form of déjà vu."

"So, is it mass hysteria?" asked Martin.

"I don't think so," replied Diane. "I think what we experience is unique to each of us, and maybe to other people we are unaware of. I don't remember the nightclub either, but based on my own experiences of things and people disappearing without others noticing, I believe Lloyd."

"So, you are suggesting that this is happening to the two of you and maybe others, but what is disappearing is unique to each individual?"

"Yes, I guess so," said Diane.

"I'll go with that also," added Lloyd.

Martin stared out the window at the top of the building next door. Suddenly, he laughed. "Did I read my calendar wrong? Is it April Fool's day? I have to hand it to you two. You really had me going for a minute. When did you cook this up?"

"We didn't cook anything up," said Diane. "I resent that you think I would do something like that."

"Oh, come on," said Martin, "I'll admit it. You had me going. No offense taken." He checked his watch. "Break time is almost up. Let's meet back here for lunch and you can fill me in on how you came up with this. Let me clear the table."

"Go ahead, we'll catch up," said Lloyd.

Martin gathered the cans and bottles, leaving Diane and Lloyd at the table deep in conversation. He stopped at the door, depositing them into the waiting recycling bin. He turned, expecting to see his companions, then gasped. "What the…?"

As for the others in the room, no one seemed to notice.

HÓNG'S HARDWARE[5]

Karl Müller approached the counter where ancient Hóng sat counting some coins. "I want to purchase five feet of your finest three-eighths inch manila rope and a sturdy ceiling bracket."

"What for you want rope?" asked Hóng, without looking up.

"I would say that is my business. Is this not a hardware emporium? I think I should be able to purchase what I please without your scrutiny."

Hóng looked up. "At Hóng's Hardware, we provide what you need, not what you want."

"Well then," huffed Müller, I'll have my rope and bracket."

"Five feet of rope and a ceiling bracket," mused Hóng. "Very few applications for such. Maybe you hang yourself?"

Damn you Hóng! Prying little bastard. Committing suicide is a private matter, not the subject of discussion with clerks. Think of something. "Ahhh, if you must know, I have purchased a hanging rattan settee, which I plan to install in my apartment."

"Why settee and not chair?"

"So my dog, Zeppelin, can sit with me, if you must know."

"Dog get sick swinging. How high your ceiling?" asked Hóng.

"What concern is that of yours?" huffed Müller.

"Five feet not enough rope to hang a settee. Hang you maybe, but not a settee."

Damn you Hóng! "I don't know," grumbled Müller. "Ten feet, maybe."

[5] "Hóng's Hardware" appeared online in *CafeLit*, 7/20/2021

"Then you need ten feet of rope to hang a settee," said Hóng.

"Well then, make it ten feet and throw in the bracket and anything else I might need. And be quick about it, I'm in a hurry." Müller paced while Hóng cut and coiled the rope and retrieved a bracket and some other tools.

"Make sure you mount bracket to rafter," said Hóng, as he rang up the bill on a timeworn cash register. Müller examined it, dug out his coin purse, and carefully counted out the money, which he laid on the counter.

Müller left Hóng's Hardware, walked down Franklin Street, and stepped inside Nally's Grocery.

"Top o' the morning, Karl," said Sean Nally. " What can I do for you today?"

"I would like some scraps for Zeppelin. Nothing too rich mind you. He has a sensitive stomach."

"Why not try a can of Ken-L Ration dog food?" suggested Sean. " They say it's a lot better than scraps."

"Food for dogs in a can?"

"Sure, I sell a lot of it. Wait." Sean walked down the aisle and retrieved a can from the bottom shelf. He handed the can to Müller. "Here, see for yourself."

Müller placed his sack on the counter while he read the label on the can.

"What's the rope for?" asked Sean. "Nothing sinister, I hope."

What? "Oh, I'm going to hang…" *Damn.* "Um-er-ah… hang a settee, that is. How much?" asked Müller.

"Ten cents. By the way, have you met the young widow who just moved into Ma Bates's Boarding House? Quite a looker. Her name is Nora Seidl, Austrian I think. You should ask her out."

Müller dug a dime from his change purse and handed it over. "I doubt Mrs. Seidl would be interested in the likes of me."

"Never know 'til you try."

"Good day, Sean," bid Müller, as he stepped out onto Franklin Street.

He made his way down to Number 36, staring at the sidewalk. He climbed the stairs to his top floor apartment. Zeppelin, a plump grey dachshund, got up from his spot under the window to greet Müller, who held out the parcels for inspection.

"Look what I have here," said Müller. He reached inside the sack and pulled out the can of dog food, holding it out for the dog to sniff. "Sean Nally says this is very popular. Shall we try some at supper? Then, I have something to discuss with you." Zeppelin sighed, then returned to his spot under the window.

Müller placed the dog food on the counter and laid out his purchases from Hóng's to inspect. There was the coil of rope, a sturdy bracket, some bolts, a bit and brace, and a wrench. Satisfied he had all he needed, Müller retired to his chair and read the paper.

At supper, Müller prepared some lentil soup which he ate with a crust of stale bread. He opened the dog food and scooped out a portion.

"Zeppelin, it's time to have a discussion," he said. "I have made a decision. I am going to hang myself. Do not try to convince me otherwise. I have made up my mind. You see, I have purchased all the necessary equipment. There is a ladder in the basement. Tomorrow, I will bring it up and install the bracket on the rafter up there." He pointed toward the ceiling. "Then, I will attach the rope and … well, you know.

"I have not made this decision lightly, but I just feel I have nothing to live for anymore. I just drift from day to day without

25

real purpose, isolated. Look at me, I am a balding, middle-aged man. I have no real friends. At work, I sit in my cubicle and post accounts all day." Zeppelin rolled over for a tummy rub. "And as for you, my canine companion, you are indeed a loyal and loving pet, but I need something more. But not to worry, I will leave a note with some money to take care of you. Someone will want you. I am sure you will be all right."

The next morning, Müller was awakened by a loud knock at the door. He pulled on his robe, ambling to his door. He pushed aside the cover on the speakeasy and spied two burly men.

"What is it you want?" he asked.

"Got a delivery for Müller from Hóng's Hardware."

"Must be a mistake. I ordered nothing from Hóng."

"There's a note. It says to deliver a rattan settee to Mr. Karl Müller, Number 36, top floor Franklin Street. Compliments of Hóng's Hardware." Müller stood on his toes and peered down through the speakeasy at the floor. A large crate sat at the men's feet. "So we can leave it out here or bring it in. Up to you."

Can't refuse it or Hóng will get suspicious. Müller opened the door. "Bring it in and put it by the chair." After the men left, Müller examined the crate. There was a note attached. He opened it.

'Mr. Müller, I have taken the liberty to have this rattan settee brought to you. I am sure in your haste to get your rope, you forgot to order the settee. Now, you may complete your stated task. At Hóng's Hardware, we supply what you need.

Changpu Hóng'

Zeppelin sniffed the crate. "The gall of the man," fumed Müller. "How did he know I didn't have a settee? Just a lucky

26

guess? Has he been spying on me? What right does he have to interfere in my plans? Never mind, the deed is done. I couldn't refuse it, or he would have become more suspicious. What will we do?" Müller sat down in his chair, burying his face in his hands. Zeppelin sighed and plopped down at Müller's feet.

A few minutes later, he reached down and rubbed behind Zeppelin's ear. "I know. Ein kaffee mit sahne und zucker und schnecken. And for you, a bit of knackwurst." Müller got up and brewed his coffee, added cream and sugar, and pulled a small pecan cinnamon bun from the breadbox, placing it on a napkin. He opened the icebox and cut a bit of sausage, which he placed in Zeppelin's bowl.

After they ate, Müller said, "There is only one course of action. To avert any suspicion, I will assemble the settee. That way, in case Hóng or some other nosy individual comes by, I can maintain an appearance of normalcy. Then when the time is right, I can cut the rope and hang myself." Zeppelin looked up from his bowl and groaned.

Müller prized open the crate and carefully extracted the settee. "Look how beautiful it is," he exclaimed, running his fingers over its smooth, lacquered frame and intricate Viennese braiding. He marveled at its ornate silk batik cushion. Zeppelin promptly snuggled into the soft seat. "Ah yes," said Müller, "you stay here while I go get the ladder."

Müller dragged the ladder up the four flights of stairs to his apartment. It was late in the afternoon by the time he had secured the bracket to the ceiling joist and attached the rope so the settee hung at the right height. While on the ladder, he had looked about his apartment. From his bird's eye view, he could see the dust that had accumulated over the books and newspapers haphazardly strewn about. He could see the kitchen counter overflowing with plates and glasses. He could see the piles of rumpled clothes on the bedroom floor. He climbed down and sat next to Zeppelin.

"This is no good," he said. " I can't hang myself with my apartment in this sad state. What will people think when they find me? That I had no pride? That I lived in squalor? No, tomorrow, we clean this place up."

The next day, Müller cleaned and cleaned and cleaned while Zeppelin watched from the settee. Müller had placed a towel over the cushion. "You must understand, we don't want dog hair on the seat." Müller even cleaned the large gable window. He was amazed at how much light poured in.

In the afternoon, Müller surveyed his neat and gleaming abode. "Zeppelin," he said, "I think we should celebrate this fine clean apartment. I will go to Tomasino's and get something special for supper." Zeppelin barked. Müller put on his coat and cap and headed down Franklin Street. When he reached the store, he could smell the meats and cheeses which hung throughout the small shop. He walked in. There was a young woman behind the counter.

"Good day to you, Giovanna," he said tipping his cap.

"Good day to you Mr. Müller. What can I get you?"

"I should like a round of that rustic bread…"

"The Pagnotta?" asked Giovanna.

"Yes, that's it. Now, please cut for me some Prosciutto di Parma and I'll finish up with some Castelvetrano olives ."

"Anything else? Something to drink perhaps?"

Müller peered at the wines and liqueurs. "Ah yes, some Limoncello."

"Excellent choice," said Giovanna. She retrieved a bottle of the yellow liqueur. "This is a most delicious concoction. It's made from Sorrento lemons, which are the best."

"Then I shall take it."

That evening, Müller prepared a large sandwich of Pagnotta and Prosciutto dotted with the olives. He shared the succulent ham with Zeppelin, who eagerly wolfed it down. "But not too much, for it is very rich. You know, after all my hard work, it would be a waste of effort to hang myself right away. Perhaps I should wait a while. Tomorrow, I think I will put on my good coat and go settle with Hóng. Then I shall go to Ma Bate's Boarding House and invite Mrs. Nora Seidl to supper. If she accepts, then… we'll see."

He settled into the settee and savored the Limoncello. He toasted Zeppelin, he toasted Giovanna, he toasted Sean Nally, he toasted Nora Seidl, then he toasted Hóng, finally falling asleep in the settee with Zeppelin at his side.

After breakfast the next morning, Müller donned his good coat and set out for Hóng's Hardware. He entered the store and found Hóng sitting behind the counter counting coins.

"Mr. Hóng," he said, " I've come to settle up on the settee."

"One dollar."

"Oh surely such a fine piece of furniture cost more than one dollar."

"Let's say I receive deep discount which I pass along to customer."

"Are you sure?"

"Quite sure," said Hóng.

Müller pulled out his change purse and retrieved four quarters which he laid on the counter. Hóng punched a button on the cash register and the drawer popped open. He carefully placed the quarters in the till, closed the drawer, and $1.00 appeared in the window.

"Well, thank you, Mr. Hóng. I shall be on my way," said Müller.

"One more thing, Mr. Müller, before you leave."

"What's that?"

Hóng reached under the counter and pulled out a book. He held it out to Müller. " This book for you."

"I didn't order a book."

"Of course you didn't. You are wearing your good coat. After you leave here, you plan to go to Ma Bate's Boarding House and invite Mrs. Seidl to supper at your apartment. Correct?"

"Ahhh, yes. How did you know that?" stammered Müller.

"Mrs. Seidl will accept your invitation which is why you will need book. I have marked page forty three. It contains a recipe for Wiener Schnitzel, a thin, breaded and deep fried meat dish usually made from veal..."

"I know what it is," grumbled Müller.

"It pairs well with Grüner Veltliner, a dry white wine, which is a particular favorite of Mrs. Seidl. After supper, she will be most pleased to sit next to you in the settee and listen to your lovely recording of Schumann."

Müller took the book. A feather stuck out from the pages. They opened to the recipe for Wiener Schnitzel. He looked at Hóng.

Hóng smiled and said, "At Hóng's Hardware, we provide what you need."

THE RED STAR[6]

"Vilis, stop daydreaming," Aivar called. He stood up, stretching his aching back. "If you want to see it, we need to finish digging the blueroot before nightfall."

"I wasn't daydreaming, I was looking for it."

"You'll not be able to see it until it's dark."

"Why?"

"When do you see the stars?"

"When it gets dark."

"Then, I suggest you finish your work before you look to the stars. Tonight, everyone will gather on the commons to look for it. We will join them."

"Yes Father."

* * *

Daylight had faded into dusk by the time Vilis and Aivar returned home. "Take some roots to your mother for the pot," said Aivar, lowering the handles of his cart to the ground. "I'll put the rest in the cellar." Vilis untied a gathering sack and pulled out two handfuls. He ran to the kitchen.

His mother, Liga, was peeling the skin from a toothless eel-fish when Vilis entered. He inhaled the aroma of seedgrass bread baking in the oven. Placing the vegetables on the table, he said, "Father says we will go to the commons tonight to see it."

"Not before supper and we will not have supper until those are washed," she said.

Vilis carried the vegetables to the sink. He scrubbed the knobby roots with his hands. Liga had finished gutting the eel-

---

[6] "The Red Star" appeared in *Our Universes* - a Boyle County Public Library Chapbook published through Sheppard Press, 2019.

fish by the time he brought them back to the table. She placed them on the cutting board with the eel, then chopped all into bite sized pieces before dumping them into the cooking pot.

* * *

Vilis's village perched on a bluff where rolling inland prairies of seedgrass met a wide shallow sea. Brilliant stars hovered in Lyca IV's clear night sky. Near the shore, their reflected light danced on soft waves. The reflection of the planet's two moons created a shimmering 'V' that stretched across the water toward the horizon. The tall, wispy nova wheat looked like a second sea, undulating in the ever present breezes that swept in from the water.

Vilis and his family joined the others in the area outside the village called the commons. Liga told him it was the spot where, long ago, the colonization spaceship had landed. Laughter and singing filled the night air as the villagers assembled. She spread out a large blanket, then sat down, cradling Vilis's infant sister, Rota, in her lap.

"Hand me the basket," she said to Vilis.

She opened it and retrieved the wild yellow berries she had picked earlier. She handed a bunch each to Aivar and Vilis, keeping a small portion for herself. She offered a breast to Rota who eagerly began to feed. Vilis popped a fat berry into his mouth and bit through its slightly bitter skin, allowing the sweet pulp to explode in his mouth.

"Aivar!" Ludis shouted, as he waded through the crowd. He held a large mug high above his head. Its amber contents glowed in the moons' light. Reaching Aivar, he slapped him on the shoulder with his free hand. "What say you, brother? Will you be joining us at the Golden Eel after the viewing? Zein has brewed up a new version of his awful swill in honor of tonight.

32

Calls it 'Glowing Red Ale'. More than likely, them that drink it will call it glorious red runs in the morning."

Liga glared at her brother-in-law.

"Vilis, say 'hi' to your uncle Ludis."

"Hi, Uncle Lud," Vilis said. Yellow juice rolled down his chin. "Can I have some red tail?"

Jaxon looked at Liga and sneered. Bending down close to his nephew, he said, "No, no Vil, my boy. I don't think you'd like it very much."

"Neither would your father," said Liga.

"Liga's right," said Aivar, "got to work tomorrow. Don't need to contend with the aftermath of one of Zein's concoctions in the morning. Besides, I don't really see this as a reason for celebration."

"What about all these others?" Ludis asked. "If we're not celebrating, why throw a big picnic?"

Liga's eyes flashed. "It's not a picnic," she said. "It's a gathering to remember, to take a last look. For the young ones, like Vilis and Rota, it is a chance to learn."

"Still looks like a picnic to me," muttered Ludis. "Anyhow, won't Vilis and Rota learn all about it when they start school? Ain't that why we got teachers? Anyway, all that's ancient history, I say. No need to cry over spilt milk. Why ruin a good party with education?"

Sensing the growing tension between Liga and Ludis, Aivar interjected, "How about we agree to disagree?"

"Suit yourself," Ludis said. He glanced at Liga, then took a long drink from his mug. He looked around the commons for a graceful exit. "Say, there's Karlis over there?" he said. "I need to have a word with him. So, begging your pardon, I'll take my leave." He clapped Aivar on the shoulder and nodded to Liga. "Take care."

"You too," said Aivar. He looked at Liga and smiled. "I wouldn't have gone to Zein's, you know. I gave that up when we got married."

"I know, but it seems your brother isn't aware of it."

"Keep a sharp eye out, Vilis," said Aivar, pointing across the water. "It should appear on the horizon anytime now, rising out of the sea."

"Do the stars come out of the sea?" asked Vilis.

"No, but it looks like they do. I'll explain how the stars come to fly across the sky," said Aivar, "but it'll take too long now. Remind me tomorrow and I'll tell you all about it. But now, your job is to watch."

"I see it!" someone shouted. "Just as they predicted."

"Where?" asked another.

"There to the right."

All heads turned. A murmur of excitement swirled through the crowd, which erupted into cheers and clapping.

Vilis tugged his father's hand.

"What is it, son?"

"I can't see. Everyone is standing in front of me."

Aivar lifted Vilis to his shoulders. "How's that?"

Vilis looked over the heads of the crowd as a red star broke free of the black horizon. "I see it, I see it!"

* * *

The red star, hovering overhead, gleamed in the night sky like a ruby on black velvet, studded with diamonds. Aivar lowered Vilis to the ground.

"Where'd it come from?" Vilis asked. "Why haven't we seen it before?"

"It was a star, like the other stars," said Lida, "but it became something special, a luminous red nova."

"How?"

"A very long time ago," Liga explained, "our ancestors lived on a planet that revolved around a distant star. Their scientists discovered that a wild, roaming star was going to smash into their star, causing both to explode, destroying everything, including their planet. That is why they left and came here."

"On the spaceship?" asked Vilis.

"Yes," replied Aivar.

"And so we see in the sky tonight," continued Liga, "what the scientists predicted so long ago has come to pass. This luminous red nova is all that remains of our ancestral home. Like a dying ember in the hearth fire, it will glow for a while, then fade away never to be seen again."

"What was the name of their planet?" asked Vilis.

"They called it Earth."

GRANDMA'S SEASON[7]

A blast of hot, muggy August slapped Tyler in the face as he opened the car door. It was one of those days when air conditioners ran continuously, and tar oozed out of the asphalt, sticking to shoe soles if you didn't watch where you stepped. He stood before the squat, single story building. A weather-beaten plywood sign poked out of the scrubby grass. 'Fern Manor Nursing and Rehabilitation' was painted on its surface. To him, it was just a fancy name for the final destination of the sick and forgotten. White scabs of paint peeled away from the building's aging walls revealing spalled brick. He surveyed the parking lot and grounds. *Are you here, harsh man? The other visitors and the nursing home staff may not be able to see you, but I can.*

As he approached the front door, Tyler's thoughts turned to the day, almost two years ago when they brought his Grandma Alice here after she fell and broke her hip. *I'm sorry we had to bring you here, Grandma…*

* * *

"Why can't I go back home?" asked Grandma Alice, as the aides lifted her onto the bed.

"Mom, we've been over that," said Lonny, "once you can move around on your own, you'll come to our house for a bit, then we'll see when you can go home."

"Why can't y'all take care of me?"

"Mother Alice," interjected Louise, "We've been all over that. You know Ray took that long haul job down in Knoxville. He's on the road four or five days a week. Tommy and Marie are

---

[7] "Grandma's Season" appeared online in *CommuterLit*, 3/7/2019.

ready to start school and Irene's got to stay there to take care of them. Lonny and I both got full time jobs, and Tyler has school."

"But, I took care of your Daddy at home when he got sick."

"That was different," said Lonny, "besides, I don't know if that was the best thing. He never did get well, and I think it took too much outta you, tending to him 24 hours a day and all that. Lookin' back, I think maybe we should've done something like this with him. But, it was your decision, and we went with it."

"Don't worry," she replied, "I'll only be here but a week or so till I'm up on my feet." She smiled and laughed softly, but her eyes betrayed a sadness that her best efforts could not hide.

"That's the spirit," said Lonny, looking to his wife for support, "ain't that right, honey?"

Louise nodded in halfhearted agreement. "I 'spect so."

"Don't worry Grandma Alice," Tyler said, "I'll water your plants and collect the mail 'til you get back."

"Thank you Ty. Make sure there's some gas for the mower when the boy comes round to cut the grass."

"If it don't rain, you'll be home before it'll need cutting. Now, when you are ready, I got it all planned out. You can take my room and I'll fix up a spot in the basement. "

* * *

…Tyler opened the old wooden, double door, glass panes rattling in their channels. He stepped into an aluminum security vestibule which had been added at some point. The three sided frame and glass structure protruded into the cramped lobby. He punched August's passcode into the entry pad. The lock clicked, and he stepped into the stale, suffocating atmosphere of the nursing home.

38

"Hi, Tyler," said the receptionist opening the visitor's register.

"Hi, Ms. Beatty, how're you doing today?" Tyler picked a pen from a stoneware mug emblazoned with a Spenserian 'FM' and signed in.

"Well, I'm doing just fine. Thanks for asking. I'm pretty sure she's in her room. Haven't seen her in the dining or TV room in a while." She handed him a visitor's badge.

"Thanks." he said, clipping the badge to his pocket.

Tyler walked through the large, cased opening to the right of the receptionist's desk into a main room, housing the dining and TV areas. It spanned the width of the building. *Such a sad place.*

The dining area on the left percolated the nauseating odor of Salisbury steak and bleach. Anyone passing would cause the residents to lift their heads in hopes of seeing the loved ones who never came. Are you here today harsh man? Tyler scanned the tables. *I've seen you here. You come here often, don't you. And I know who you are - what you hunger for. What do you whisper to them while they eat?*

Tyler turned his attention to the TV area. A few residents slumped in the soiled and tattered sofas and chairs while aides watched talk shows. *Or are you here?* He looked around the room. *You can't hide. Do you eventually convince them all to leave with you?*

After she first arrived, Tyler would often find Grandma Alice in the dining room or watching TV. As the months passed, however, she gradually withdrew from these activities and took to spending more time in her room. All the while, she grew weaker; in the last few months she had become bedridden.

39

Ahead, a wheelchair bound resident waited in the aisle while an aide readied a dining table for her. *Have you seen the harsh man? I have. It was only a few months after Grandma was admitted. Ms. Beatty had fussed at me about my visitor badge...*

* * *

"How long have you been coming here? Three months, I bet, and you still can't remember to turn in your badge?"

"Yeah, that's about right," Tyler said, pulling the badge from his shirt and handing it over.

"And you still forget."

"I guess so," Tyler sighed. "Got a lot on my mind."

"How's Ms. Alice doing?"

"Not very well, I think."

"Well, don't give up too soon," she said. "Sometimes they'll surprise you." She tapped a button on her desk and the lock clicked open.

"Thanks Ms. Beatty."

Tyler stepped out into the fall afternoon. The air was crisp and he was thankful to breathe in some cool, fresh air. A tall, gaunt figure dressed in a black serge suit stood on the sidewalk. His white shirt was buttoned at the collar. A black fedora sat atop his thin yellow-white hair. The suit appeared to be freshly pressed, creases sharp as razors. A breeze rattled his trousers around his thin legs. Boney hands protruded from his coat sleeves, each finger punctuated with a long amber nail. His jet black eyes were trained on Tyler. The skin of his face was harsh and blotchy, pulled taught over high cheekbones such that his lips were drawn open revealing long teeth the color of old ivory.

Tyler was so unnerved by the harsh countenance of the man, he veered off the sidewalk and ran across the lawn to avoid passing him. Safely in his car, Tyler jammed the key in the ignition and hit the gas, almost sideswiping the car parked next to his. As he shot out of the parking lot, Tyler glanced in the rearview mirror. The harsh man was gone.

* * *

…Tyler walked around the woman in the wheelchair toward the narrow opening which led into the green corridor and eventually into the residents' hall. As much as he had come to dislike walking through the main room, Tyler dreaded entering the green corridor; the long stretch that serviced the kitchen, laundry and utility rooms followed by the janitor's closet and the aides workstation. The stale odor of soiled linen and disinfectant permeated the dim hallway. The dementia sufferers were stowed in this area while the aides changed linens or sat in the breakroom eating and arguing over who would have to answer the next bell.

Are you in there harsh man? It's one of your favorite spots. How often do you linger there, sucking the last bit of coherent thought from those helpless minds? Tyler stopped at the threshold, peering down the corridor. Steeling himself, he stepped forward, trying not to make eye contact.

At first, before he knew better, he would look at patients strapped in their wheelchairs or, even worse, say a kind word to one. The result was always the same. Once eye contact was made, or a word uttered, they would begin to shout, shake, or pound their fists. The cacophony would swell until it overwhelmed Tyler.

He had learned his lesson. So carefully, Tyler walked on; the walls and ceiling closing in on him and the air thickening in his lungs. Each footstep sounded like a clap of thunder. Do they blame me for their suffering? He started to tiptoe. *If I get too close, will one grab me?* He drew his arms close to his body. *Will the others join, screaming, biting me with sharp teeth, suffocating me*

41

in their dark breath? Will they gnaw away my youth, leaving only frail, mottled parchment to cover my brittle bones? Then, after the aides have tied me in a wheelchair, will the harsh man come for me? Fighting his fear, he continued until he reached the doorway to the residential hall. From there, it was six doors down to Grandma Alice's room.

Tyler stood outside her room for a few moments to compose himself. Intellectually, he knew death, even for Grandma Alice, was inevitable. In his soul, he longed to find a way to ward it off. For him, the process of death was mysterious and frightening; something from which he had always been sheltered. It was something cloaked in dark secrets whispered by his parents when they thought he was out of earshot. He could only guess about the process of death. It terrified him.

Tyler took a deep breath then entered and sat down in the chair between Grandma Alice's bed and the window. He carefully avoided touching the exposed wood, sticky with the buildup of body oils and furniture polish.

"How are you feeling today?" he asked. She remained still, eyes seemingly focused on something beyond him in the distance.

An aide poked her head in the door. "Don't she look pretty? We just gave her a bath and washed her hair this mornin'. Put fresh linens on her bed too."

"Thanks," said Tyler. "She say anything?"

"Sometimes she does. Sometimes, she talks to the angels."

"What's that?"

"That's when she gets that faraway look in her eyes and she whispers things. Like she is talking to the angels. When it gets close to the end, a lot of them do it."

"What does she say?"

"Oh, most of the time she whispers so soft you can't understand what she's saying. I need to roll her over."

"Can you give me a few minutes; I won't be long."

"Take all the time you need. I'll come back later."

"Thanks." Tyler looked at Grandma Alice. *I know who it is. It's not the angels.*

* * *

A month later, Tyler returned to Fern Manor. The October sun gleamed in a cloudless blue sky and the bursts of red, yellow, and gold fall foliage were at their peak. They reminded him that his Grandma had always said fall was her favorite season. He remembered how she had loved to go for a drive to see the fall colors. He feared this would be her last.

He scanned the parking lot. *Where are you harsh man?* As he walked to the entrance, he stopped to gather some of the colorful leaves just fallen from the trees. Maybe these would spark something in her; brighten her day.

Tyler checked in with Ms. Beatty, then started his journey to Grandma Alice's room. The atmosphere in the dining and assembly areas seemed lighter. The residents were quietly watching TV or eating their lunches. He managed to navigate the patient wheelchairs without drawing the attention of their occupants.

He found Grandma Alice sleeping quietly in her bed. He took her frail hand.

"Grandma Alice, can you hear me? It's Tyler. I brought some fall leaves for you." He placed them on the nightstand by the bed. He leaned in close and kissed her forehead, then whispered, "Love you."

She opened her eyes. They were fixed on the doorway. Tyler looked up and gasped. The harsh man was standing in the threshold, his eyes fixed on Grandma Alice. Tyler couldn't move, heart pounding harder than it ever had. *I won't let you in...* He straightened up and faced the harsh man. *...no matter what you do to me.* Tyler's feet froze in place as if cemented to the floor. His head began to spin into unconsciousness when he felt a soft touch on his arm.

"You must be Alice's grandson," she said in a soft, musical voice.

Immediately, he regained his equilibrium. He looked to his side. A small woman who looked to be in her seventies came into focus. Her hand had a pleasantly calming effect on Tyler, and for a moment, the terror he was experiencing left. *Where did you come from?* Her eyes sparkled robin's egg blue, a deep smile filled her face. She was dressed in the fashion of the flower ladies who perform volunteer work in the hospitals.

"How do you know me?" he stammered. *How did you get here?*

"Oh, I've been visiting with Alice for some time now. We've had many conversations. She is such a lovely person." The flower lady gently tugged on his arm. "Do you have a moment that we could talk?"

"I can't," he said, glaring at the harsh man, still lurking in the doorway. *Is this one of your tricks?*

"No it isn't," said the flower lady. "Pay him no mind; nothing will happen until you are ready."

"But I don't understand... "

"Exactly, and that is why we need to talk. You must trust me when I say that nothing will happen until after that. See he's gone." Tyler looked up to see the doorway was empty. She led him out into the hallway. "Trust," she said.

They walked through the doors at the end of the hall into the courtyard just outside. Tyler wanted to resist, but could not. In the dimming sunlight of the autumn afternoon, she led him to a wrought iron bench.

"You've kept a long and arduous vigil on your grandmother," she began, "and now it's time to let her go. As the seasons pass, so must our lives; and your grandmother's season now comes to its end." Her words stung Tyler; but also eased some of his fear and anxiety. He thought back to Grandma Alice's room with the harsh man standing in the doorway.

"I won't let her go with him. I know who he is. Death! He is death, come for Grandma. Alice. He is old and angry, resentful of the living. His only consolation is to take others into his misery. I can't let her go. Not with him. Not like that!"

The flower lady looked right into Tyler's soul.

"Oh, you are mistaken, Tyler. He is not death, he is life. Life that has reached its conclusion. Life that is ready to rest. Life that has lingered too long in its autumn, restless to sleep. Life ready for its rebirth."

"No!"

"Trust me Tyler, it's true."

"How can I be sure?" he asked.

"Your grandmother loved the fall. She reveled in the harvest of the fruits of spring and summer. She treasured the last days of autumn's beauty before the white sleep of winter. She knew that the promise of autumn and the work of winter is the glory of new life in the spring. Now she is ready to pass on to a new life. One beyond your comprehension. A life of unbound beauty and joy. Consider. Would you make the trees hold their dead leaves so they could not rest? Would you halt the cycle of nature? I think not. Why, then, would you hold your Grandma Alice back?"

Tyler sat still for some time watching the leaves fall, letting the significance of the flower lady's words settle into his soul. He knew she was right, not because he reasoned it; but, because he felt it in his heart. The terror of Grandma Alice's death evaporated and with that, the weight of fear floated away like a leaf in the autumn wind. He understood he must let her go. He would miss her always and grieve for his loss, but he understood it was the way it was meant to be. He turned to thank the flower lady, but she was gone.

The ward nurse opened the door and stepped into the courtyard.

"I thought I saw you come out here," she said in a solemn voice. Tyler knew the words before she spoke them. "Your grandmother has just expired. I'm so sorry, she was such a wonderful person."

Tyler thanked her and walked back to Grandma Alice's room. As he entered, he could see the harsh man standing at the head of her bed. His face softened, taking on a tranquil look, and his eyes closed as he disappeared into the shadows.

Tyler looked down at Grandma Alice. She was at peace and he knew the flower lady would take good care of her.

WORTH THE WAIT

"What's this place you're taking us to?" Jaxon asked.

"It's a surprise. They say there's nothing like it anywhere," said Aria.

"Not even Pokémon Galaxy above Old Tokyo?" asked Jaxon. "I fact the whole thing floats over the rubble. Wish we coulda' transpose there."

"Be maglev. Alias another fancy arcade. You could eye the same giz in the underground caverns of Lost Vegas. Wish they'd let you bring your oPad so you wouldn't have to fuss with paper." She pulled the brochure from her pocket. It was limp from perspiration. She studied its contents, fingers sticking to its glossy surface.

"Where do they even get stuff to make that anymore?" asked Jaxon.

"Landfill mines maybe. They printed this up as part of the do it, I guess. Used to be, they had paper info like this for everything. Called bro sures. I'm not sure what that meant. Anyway, must'a been a real ick-fest."

"And what's with the noise?" Jaxon asked, pointing to the speakers in the canopy. "It's been giving me a headache for three hours now."

"I think it's twentieth century music called rocken droll. Untenable, but it kinda goes with the bro sures."

"No oPads, no vid displays, rocken droll, " whined Jaxon. He stared at the wall with 'Old York Excursions' stenciled on it. "Nothing to eye at but the stupid walls and the other forty-eight miserable slogs in here. Smells like old socks."

The speakers went silent, then crackled before the metallic voice said, "Magcoach is about to advance. Magcoach is about to advance." Inertia tugged them down as they levitated.

"Here we go!" said Aria. "I think we're there."

"If only I had a hundred credits for every time I've eared that today. Tell me again, how much did this go about cost?" Jaxon grumbled.

Aria grimaced. "Three month's credits."

"Well, then I could pay you back and we could go about to Pokémon Galaxy and Lost Vegas and still have protein loaf and champagne for supper." Jaxon squirmed against his safety harness. "I've been strapped down on this bench for three hours. I think my butt's sprouted roots."

"Yeah, yeah, yeah, but I told you this is a once in a lifetime get to. The only way to access tickets is to win a get in lottery. Cost five hundred credits for a chance to win one get in, a thousand for a chance to win two. I been trying for ten years. You should consider yourself lucky. I asked you to come with me . . . as my date. I've got plenty of girlfriends who would have happily trans out epic credits for my anda ticket."

"Well, there's only about a million lotteries going on. Maybe if I knew where the hell we're going, I might get jubed."

The magcoach fluttered a moment before it settled. "The magcoach has stopped. The magcoach has stopped."

To their left, the doors slid open and their safety harnesses released. The speakers crackled again. "Lenox Station. Lenox Station."

"Hurry," said Aria standing up, "the doors are about to close." Jaxon glared at her.

They queued up with the other passengers, exiting into a dimly lit, cramped vestibule while another group entered from the right to replace them. At the other side of the small room was an archway. As soon as the magcoach door whisked shut, the lights in the tunnel beyond blinked on, accompanied by the soft rumble of gears and belts. Speakers in the tunnel announced, "The travellator is moving. Please hold the handrail. The travellator is moving. Please hold the handrail." Instinctively, Aria, Jaxon and the other passengers stepped single file onto the moving conveyor.

While they moved through the tunnel, the metallic voice repeated, "For your safety, remain on the travellator at all times." After a few minutes, the message changed. "The travellator terminates ahead, please step off and move forward."

"We coulda been lipping Moscow Mules in Underground Atlanta right now," Jaxon said, stumbling off the travellator.

"I think we're here," Aria said, grabbing his arm. "I see the gondolas just ahead."

"Gone to whats?"

"Gondolas, those little tub things we're going to ride in. You shoulda read your bro sure."

"Who needs a bro sure with you around?"

A set of bright yellow gondolas whisked down a tunnel to the right as they entered a rectangular room bisected by a railing to their left. A uniformed guide handed them a mask saying, "Welcome to Lenox Station. The gondolas will be here shortly. Move straight ahead. You may line up, two persons to a car."

Another guide made sure they were lined up in pairs between the yellow lines at the edge of the loading dock. A recorded message blared over the speakers. "Wait until the gondola has stopped before entering. Please fasten your seat belt. Remain seated at all times until the gondola has returned. Place your mask firmly over your nose and mouth, secure the elastic band behind your head, and breathe normally. Do not remove your mask until your gondola has returned. Enjoy."

Twenty five fuchsia gondolas popped out from a tunnel to the left, stopping at the unloading dock on the other side of the railing. The passengers got off and the gondolas swept forward, stopping neatly in front of Aria and Jaxon's group. After they piled on, fastened their seat belts and donned their masks, the gondolas swooped off down a dark corridor.

They moved through the dark until they burst out into an immense enclosure bathed in sunlight. The surface below was covered in a thousand shades of green, interrupted only by some irregular patches of blue and the concrete walls around the perimeter. The whole enclosure was capped by a crystal dome.

"What is this?" Jaxon gasped.

"Jaxon, you're eying the last 3.4 square kilometers of grass and trees left in North America. In the way back, they called it Central Park."

PERCEIVED TOGETHER[8]

Jaron walked at a brisk pace through the park. Fat snowflakes drifted all around him on their gentle journey. There was just enough early morning light and landmarks protruding from the thick blanket of snow to guide him. He hoped to have an hour or two before the children finished their oatmeal and cartoons. After that, they would arrive to fill the day with their kaleidoscope of sound and color.

He worked his way along the flat ridge. A hundred yards to his right, the ground dropped away sharply like a waterfall until it spilled out into a wide valley. For the adventurous, a number of switchback hiking trails twisted their way down through scrub vegetation to the valley floor. A roughhewn log bench sat at each trailhead.

To the left, the slope was much more gradual, forming the perfect sledding venue for snowy days. Soon, parks and rec would set up their kerosene salamanders. Since this was a snow day for the local schools, the youthful sledders would be that much more enthusiastic in their celebration of good fortune. More enthusiasm meant more noise and its resultant firework displays.

Jaron had nothing against the panoply of colors produced by the ordinary sounds of life. On the contrary, for the most part he found them a pleasant experience, even though he was quite used to it. He started seeing the colors during childhood and developed his gift, as he had come to consider it, at the same time he learned to harness his other senses. Now it was as much of his regular life as any other aspect. Like a sailor who learns to walk with the roll and pitch of his ship, it became second nature. Even

---

[8] "Perceived Together" appeared online in *CafeLit*, 4/13/2018.

so, he kept his gift a well-hidden secret, learning as a child such gifts often garnered ridicule.

A quiet, snow-laden morning in the park provided a rare opportunity for Jaron to enjoy his gift in a different way. Few, if any, people would be there. Fewer people meant fewer sounds. It allowed Jaron to hear the small sounds, to see the delicate and fine-grained colors so often overwhelmed by the stifling noise of humans. Each step he took produced a scrunch which sent an almost imperceptible orange puff rolling across the white. It existed only in the moment of the sound before dissolving as quickly as it originated. Even the snowflakes falling on the dead leaves in the pin oaks produced a sound which in turn gave birth to faint halos of fuchsia, barely larger that the flakes themselves. In these situations, Jaron most appreciated his hidden sense. He could experience each color in its entirety without encroachment from all the other sounds.

Jaron stopped at the rotting signpost which marked the side trail to his favorite spot. A vertical "MOCKINGBIRD TRAIL" was carved into its side. Tiny drifts of snow rested in cavities at the bottom of each letter. He was not going hiking, only to the bench where he could sit and enjoy the snow and the relative quiet it brought.

Hearing a yelp as a red flash whisked past, he turned. About 20 yards back, someone was in the snow, rolling onto their back. Peeved that his quiet, snowy morning had been interrupted, he watched, waiting to see what happened. The person did not get up, but Jaron thought he detected some movement. He quickly retraced his steps to get a closer look, his footsteps scrunching out orange puffs in profusion as he approached. Arms and legs were flailing in the snow, kicking up green swirls. Fearing the person could be injured, he picked up the pace, sending out more bright orange plumes. Soon, he was close enough to see the iridescent blue globs popping like bubbles, while he heard a woman giggling. Upon closer examination, he saw she was making a snow angel.

Jaron hesitated, not moving, not saying a word, taking it all in. Iridescent colors were a rare commodity. He stood awestruck as the colors danced against the white pallet of falling snow. The blobs dissolved as the woman stopped mid-giggle, realizing a stranger was standing over her. "Oops," she said, hot pink sparks flashing.

"I didn't mean to startle you, thought you might have fallen and hurt yourself," said Jaron.

The woman felt a soft, comforting melody roll over her. Caught off guard, she said dreamily, "Your music is beautiful,"

"What?"

Suddenly aware of what she had said, she replied amidst more hot pink, "Oh, nothing. It was nothing. I slipped and not wanting to let all this magnificent snow go to waste, decided to make a snow angel. I guess a grown woman looks pretty silly making a snow angel."

"I heard you say 'your music' as plain as day," said Jaron, a woodwind quintet carrying his voice.

"I did?"

"Yes."

"Of course I did," she admitted, sending amber shimmers floating by Jaron. "I'm sorry, it's not often I hear such wonderful music when someone speaks to me. People don't understand about the music. They think I'm a kook when I talk about it. That's why I try to keep it hidden. I'm Iris. Help me up?" she asked, extending a mittened hand through the whirling colors. "Careful, we don't want to mess up my angel."

Jaron took her hand, pulling her straight up to her feet. Iris stepped out of the snow angel, careful not to disturb the snowbound engraving. "Well done!" said Jaron, accompanied by a brass ensemble. The sound sent shivers through Iris. "I'm Jaron by the way. Now tell me about this music."

"I'm too embarrassed."

"Don't be."

She did not say anything. Her eyes searched his face, looking for how he might react if she told him about the music. In that moment, they were just two people standing in the falling snow, surrounded by silence and white. "For me, sounds create music. I call it music, though it's not really music like a tune on the radio. Just tone colors. Most of the time, only a single timbre, but on occasion more. When that happens, sometimes they blend - sometimes they don't. But every sound creates its own tone color. It's only there when the sound is present. Your music, however, is altogether different. It has rhythm, harmony, and melody - a true voice the likes of which I haven't heard before." Jaron watched a gossamer veil of teal, tinged with gold and magenta, undulate around them. He had never experienced anything like that until now. She continued, "You see, as a very young child, I had no idea this experience was unusual until I realized others did not hear music like I did. My parents dismissed it, likening it to an 'imaginary friend.' Playmates teased me until I learned to keep my gift to myself. You can imagine how boyfriends reacted once I told them." The teal morphed into a deep purple. She fell silent and the world turned white.

"At least you had the courage to try."

"Easy for you to say."

"Not as easy as you would imagine," he said, accompanied by the baritone voices of a trombone and cello. "I

54

think it would be a great burden to keep such a gift hidden as a relationship grew – so much so, it would be doomed to failure. And if the prospect of bearing such a burden prevented one from even trying, surely that would be even worse."

"So now it's patronize the kooky woman, in hopes she won't pull out her axe and start hacking away?"

"On the contrary. At least you tried to connect. Me, I could never muster the courage." He spoke in a plaintive whisper, carried on a caprice of woodwinds. "I never thought I would find someone who could comprehend my gift."

"Now, you're just having fun at my expense," Iris said, amidst a whorl of crimson tinged with indigo. "So you can hear the music?"

"No. I don't hear the music, but I see the colors."

"Colors?"

"Yes, the colors. They're my gift. Much the same as sounds create your music, sounds create my colors. Perhaps we're both genetic anomalies, or maybe the gods just thought to play a prank on us. Who knows? I might even be in a padded room and this is all just a hallucination. It makes no difference to me. All I know is the here and now. You hear music, I see colors. I see your colors. More beautiful and thrilling than any I have ever experienced. Like you, they're too good to pass up." The music was reaching full orchestration. "Come," said Jaron, extending his hand. "There is a fine spot up ahead, just off the beaten path. It has a passably comfortable bench and a magnificent view. If my music lives up to your colors, as I pray it does, sit with me before the sounds of the world catch up with us. We will talk. I will experience your aurora borealis and you, my symphony."

THE GREY[9]

"How much has it dropped?" asked Henry.

"Three quarters of an inch. It's down to ninety-two inches above the floor," replied his wife, Jenna. She was standing on a desk chair near the door inside the small attic they had converted into a bedroom. Holding the candle close to the wall, she examined the scale Henry had marked there three days earlier when the smooth grey appeared below the surface of the ceiling. "Why we got to wait until it's pitch black to do this?"

"Cause we got other things to do while it's still light out."

She ran her finger up the wall until it almost touched the grey, which was mere inches above her head. She was aware of its sharp, pungent odor. Something like the smell of wet stone but menacing. She moved the candle close to the thing above her head. Small, almost imperceptible swirls briefly snaked along its surface before disappearing into the depths above her head. Dense and impenetrable, it reminded her of the fog that hung low in the holler on cool fall mornings.

"Careful!" shouted Henry. "Don't touch the grey."

"I know," huffed Jenna. "If you're so concerned, why didn't you climb up on this chair and take a look?"

"Cause if I stood on that chair my head'd go right up into the grey."

"You could crouch down," said Jenna.

"Well, you're up there now. No need to argue. How much did you say it dropped yesterday?"

"One inch."

"Mebbe it's slowin' down," said Henry.

---

[9] "The Grey" appeared online in *Teleport Magazine*, 10/15/2020.

"Mebbe, mebbe not. Hand me a ruler."

"What for?"

"Cause I wanna try somethin'. Like an experiment." Jenna leaned down holding the candle over the desk. "Can you see?"

"Yeah," Henry said, pulling the desk drawer open. He rummaged around until his fingers found a long flat object. He pulled out an old yellow plastic ruler with stencils of the alphabet molded into the center. "Got this back in grade school," he said, handing it up to Jenna. "What ya gonna do with it? She took the ruler without responding and pushed it into the grey above her head until only the letters A-L were visible. It pierced the smooth surface without creating any disturbance. She let go and it remained suspended above her head. "What you go and do that for? Can you pull it out?"

"I don't know, but I can try." She grasped the end of the ruler and gave a tug. It did not budge. She pulled harder, careful not to break the plastic. Still it did not move. "I guess not. We'll have to see what it looks like tomorrow." She handed the candle to Henry, then hopped down from the chair.

"That's interestin'. Yesterday while I was out, I threw a rock up into the grey," said Henry. "It never come down. The grey just sucked it up. I don't know if it is floatin' up there somewhere or it just disappeared. By the way, if you was gonna do somethin' like that, next time use somethin' of yours."

"You think it really matters?" she snarled. "Besides, who knows what the grey is likely to do? It could come tumblin' down on top of us without a moment's notice."

Well, you got a point there. If it done that, then it wouldn't matter much anyhows, would it? Speakin' of such things, mebbe we should take the mattress downstairs?"

"I don't see why we can't sleep in our bedroom. The grey hasn't fallen too far. It's still way above our heads,"

"You're the one that said we don't know what the grey is likely to do," said Henry. "You really willin' to take a chance that it won't suddenly come tumblin' down on top of us while we're sleepin' and ain't got no chance to get away?"

"But it ain't done nothin' like that yet. It's been slow and steady," said Jenna. "We measured it and it only came down a half inch since yesterday."

"Three quarters," corrected Henry.

"You see, that's what I'm talkin' about. It ain't never come down more than that in a day and…and…" her voice broke off in tears.

Henry wrapped his arms around her. "Come on Jen, might as well do it now while we got enough head room."

Henry and Jenna wrestled the mattress down the stairs and into the living room. They pushed furniture up against the walls to make room.

* * *

For breakfast the next morning, Jenna boiled two eggs she had retrieved from the hen house while Henry picked the mold off the last two hot dog buns that had been languishing in the bread box. Dull light like an overcast dusk seeped through the kitchen window. "Think the sun is still up there somewhere?" she asked.

"I reckon so," said Henry, looking at his watch. "It was pitch black an hour ago and this is about the time the sun would be up. Somethin' to be thankful for, I guess."

"That and the fact there's still some propane in the tank and water in the cistern," she added. "Least till the grey gets it."

"We got some gas left to run the generator too, if we need it," reminded Henry.

"Well, if we got some gas, why don't we just fill up the truck and get outta here?" snapped Jenna. "At least we might find some food in Beckly."

"Don't you remember the President said we oughta stay at home. They said the grey was ever'where all around the world. Didn't you see them pictures of folks goin' crazy on the TV? They was fightin' and burnin' things up and the cops couldn't do nothin'. We don't want to get caught up in all that, do we?"

"That was a couple a weeks ago. There ain't been no TV or radio since. We got to try somethin' or are we just gonna sit here and get sucked up by that stuff?"

"We still got enough to get by for a while," said Henry. "Besides, no matter which way you go, you got to go uphill to get out of this valley. I bet the grey has sat right down on the blacktop. Remember watchin' them birds fly up into the grey? We never saw a one of 'em come back down, did we?"

* * *

That evening, Jenna twisted the dusty lid off a jar of bread and butter pickles she had found in the back of a cabinet and poured them over some white beans. "That takes care of the canned goods," she said.

Henry lit the solitary candle on the kitchen table. "It goes dark so fast, don't it? Like flippin' a switch," he muttered.

"What was that?" Jenna asked, setting the bowl of beans and pickles next to his plate.

"Sure woulda liked a nice hamburger to go under them pickles."

"Still got some mustard if you want. You could pretend."

"Naw, I'm fine."

Jenna slumped down in her chair across from Henry. She propped her elbows on the table and let her face fall into her hands. She sucked in a deep breath. "Are we gonna die, Henry?"

"We all die sooner or later, Jen."

"That's not what I mean, and you know it," sniffed Jenna. "I mean are we gonna die right here?"

"That may happen, or it may not. The important thing is we can't give up hope."

"Hope for what?" whimpered Jenna, wiping the tears from her eyes. "I'm too damn tired to hope. What are we just sittin' here for? Why don't we do somethin' instead of waitin' for the grey to take us?"

"What would you suggest?" asked Henry.

"I don't know, but I feel like we ought to be doin' somethin' besides sittin' here."

"Well, while there's still enough light durin' the day, there's the garden to work and the chickens to tend so we still got eggs to eat. We'll need them vegetables when harvest time comes. I can still till the low fields to get 'em ready for plantin'."

"You really think we'll be here when it's time to be pickin' beans an' tomatoes?"

"You asked what we could be doin'? That's what I think. Hell, all this scares me too, but it don't do no good frettin' about it."

Jenna fell silent for a few moments before asking, "Henry, what'd we ever do to deserve this?"

"What you mean?"

"Think maybe the grey is God's punishment? Like the plagues in Egypt."

"Punishment for what?" barked Henry. "We ain't done nothing to deserve a punishment."

"But it's got to be a reason why this is happenin'."

"You can't be worryin' about *why* it is until you know *what* it is."

"Well what is it then?" asked Jenna

"I don't know if anyone's figured that out. We don't know if this is somethin' sent from God or its that climate thing the environmental folks has been yammerin' about. Mebbe its some fool government experiment gone bad or something the terrorists has done. Hell, it could be aliens for all we know."

"Aliens?"

"Mebbe it's what killed off the dinosaurs. They ain't really figured that out for certain. They say this old rock has been around for several billion years. Best anyone can figure is that ever now and then everthin' gets killed off. Like the earth was wipin' the slate clean and gettin' a fresh start. The scientists got their ideas of what happened, but they don't know for sure. Mebbe the world has decided it's fed up and brought on the grey to wipe the slate clean. Now, can I eat in peace."

They ate the rest of their meager supper in silence. After the plates were cleaned, they went out and sat on the front porch.

Jenna blew out the candle she was holding. "Only seen black like this one time," she said.

"When was that?"

"Our eighth grade class took a trip to Mammoth Cave. Once we was deep down inside, the guide cut off the lights to show us what complete darkness really was."

"Was you scared?"

"Of course not," giggled Jenna. "I was holdin' Billy Campbell's hand."

"Never did like him much," growled Henry. He pawed around until he found Jenna's hand and squeezed it. "You scared now?"

"No, but I find it a wonderment not to see the moon or the stars."

"Or the sun for that matter," added Henry.

"Do you think we'll ever see them again?" asked Jenna.

"I'm gonna say yeah."

* * *

Two days later, Henry and Jenna were just finishing a sparse breakfast of boiled seed corn when they heard a thump accompanied by the crisp sound of shattering glass.

"What's that?" asked Jenna.

"I dunno," said Henry. "Sounded like it come from upstairs somewhere. Better go take a look. You been upstairs to see how far down the grey has come since we checked it last time?"

"No, I ain't too keen on goin' up there. No need seekin' out bad news, I say."

"I better go see what happened. Maybe some animal has got in." Henry grabbed the candle and matches and headed for the door.

"Wait for me," said Jenna.

They walked down the hall to the stairwell leading to their attic bedroom. A dull grey rectangle of light floated in the doorway at the top. Jenna wrapped her hands around Henry's arm. He could feel her trembling.

"Don't worry, Jen, it probably ain't nothin'."

The worn wooden treads creaked as they ascended the steps in the gloom and entered the room. In the frail light from

63

the small window in the gable, they could see the ceiling fan at the far end had fallen to the floor, shattering its globe.

"There's what made all the noise," said Henry.

"I can see that," said Jenna, "but what would cause it to suddenly fall?"

"Guess I better take a look," said Henry. As he stepped forward his foot landed on something. It cracked under his weight. He reached down and picked up two pieces of the yellow ruler Jenna had stuck in the grey a few days before. "That's odd."

"Lemme see." Jenna held out her hand. Henry handed over the pieces. "Light the candle so's I can see." Henry placed the candle on the desk and lit it. Jenna laid the two pieces of the ruler down in the flickering amber light. "This is the half that was stickin' outta the grey," she said. "You busted it in two when you stepped on it."

"You sure?"

"Yes, see there's only the letters A through L. That's what I left stickin' out of the grey. Think it got knocked off when the fan fell?"

"Naw, too far away." Henry picked up the pieces and studied them closely. "So, you stuck it in the grey up to the L?"

"Yeah."

"It sure don't look like it was broke off," Henry said, rubbing his finger along the end. "And it don't feel like it. This end is as smooth as the other." He handed the pieces to Jenna. "Let's check out the fan." He picked up the candle and they walked over to the fan, glass crunching under their feet as they got close. Henry handed Jenna the candle and picked up the fan, examining the downrod.

"Looks like it was cut in two," said Jenna.

"That it does." He rubbed his thumb over the end of the downrod. "It ain't dented or scratched up. There's no burrs like you would get if you cut it with a hacksaw. And the wires are cut clean off too."

"How could that happen?"

"I dunno, your guess is as good as mine. It's a sure bet this and the ruler weren't broke off, but as to what could cut them so clean, I ain't got a clue. Gimme the candle." Jenna handed it over and he held it close to the grey. His eyes searched all around the smooth surface.

"What is it?" asked Jenna. "What do you see?"

"That's just it. I don't see nothin'. The other end of the downrod should be up there, but it ain't. It's like it was never there."

"So, the grey has dropped down an' covered it up."

"So quick? That thing just fell a few minutes ago," said Henry. "We ain't seen the grey move that fast."

"We could check the wall and see how much it's come down."

"Good idea."

They went back over to the chair. Jenna hopped up on the seat and Henry handed her the candle. She held it close to the wall and followed the handwritten numbers upward until a narrow gap between the wall and the grey came into view. She let out a gasp, toppling backward. Henry broke her fall as the candle tumbled to the floor.

"You okay?" he asked, holding her tightly.

"It's gone! The damn wall is gone!" she stammered.

"What do you mean, the wall is gone? I see it right in front of my eyes."

"Not the whole wall. Just up there near the grey. There's a thin slice missin'."

"The candle is playin' tricks on your eyes. The wall just goes up in the grey."

"It may have a day or two ago, but it don't no more. If you don't believe me, get up on that chair and see for yourself."

"I'll do just that." Henry relit the candle and stepped up on the chair, careful not to stand straight up. When he held the light close to where the wall and grey intersected, he saw a narrow void just below the grey. He opened his pocketknife and probed the gap being careful not to touch the grey. "I'll be damned!"

"Believe me now?"

"What was the last measurement you took?" he asked.

"Ninety-two inches."

Henry studied the scale. "That's just where the wall ends." He stepped down from the chair. He wrapped his arms around Jenna. "Know what that means?"

"What?"

"That means the grey might be goin' back up. Maybe it'll disappear altogether."

"But what about the wall?" asked Jenna.

"We'll deal with that if and when it happens," said Henry. "Besides, I'd rather have a missin' bit of wall than have the grey keep comin' down on our heads, wouldn't you?"

"I guess so."

* * *

The next day, they climbed the creaking stairs to their bedroom. Henry stepped up on the chair. The gap extending along every wall had grown wide enough for him to stick his arm in without touching the grey. He tentatively reached in.

"Careful!" gasped Jenna.

"Don't worry." Henry said, pulling his arm out. He raised his head until his eyes were level with the gap. "You can look right through to the outside."

"What ya see?" asked Jenna.

"Can't see much, but it looks like the wall is clean cut off inside and out right where the grey stopped." He stepped down from the chair and walked over to the tiny gable window. "Well, I'll be. Look here, Jen." Jenna stepped in beside Henry.

She drew a deep breath. "Looks like everthin' has been clean cut off."

* * *

Two weeks later, Henry and Jenna were sitting on the porch after supper. At Jenna's insistence, they had spent the last three days rigging a makeshift shelter over half of the roofless attic. Henry cobbled some crude rafters from lumber he had in the barn then covered them with some plastic drop cloths. He put his arm around her and pulled her close. "You happy now you got your roof?"

"It's only half a roof, but yeah."

"Know what?"

"What?"

"The grey's been liftin' every day near as I can tell," said Henry. "At least 15 or 20 feet by now. Hasn't stopped one time. Instead, it seems like it's movin' faster all the time. Think I'll gas up the truck and see how far towards Beckly I can get. You interested in keepin' me company?"

"Really?" Jenna squealed, hugging Henry for all she was worth. She jumped up and started to dance on the porch. She sat back down and hugged Henry again. "I won't be able to sleep tonight."

"You can stay up all you like, but don't keep me awake."

"You think we gonna make it, Henry?"

"I think we got an awfully good chance, Jen. Remember when I told you the important thing was we couldn't give up hope?"

"Yeah. Think we'll see the Sun again?"

"I think we will and sooner that you expect."

"Really, I hope you're right," sighed Jenna.

"Come on, let's get ready for bed. Got a big day ahead of us tomorrow."

"Henry, can we do one more thing?"

"What's that?" asked Henry.

"Take the mattress back upstairs."

"Honey, I'm wore out."

"I know but gettin' that mattress back upstairs would start to make it feel real."

"Make what real?"

"Like we're gonna make it," said Jenna.

"What if it rains?"

"It ain't rained since the grey came. So, if it rained, that would mean the grey was gone, an' wouldn't we be happy."

Henry smiled. "That we would. Come on, you do the pullin' and I do the pushin'." He took Jenna's hand and led her inside the house.

* * *

The next morning, Henry awoke to Jenna's shouts. "Wake up, Henry! Wake up!" She bounced on her knees in the bed while shaking his shoulders. He rolled over and opened his eyes to blinding light streaming through the cloudy plastic sheeting.

"What the hell?" he croaked, struggling to clear his head from sleep.

"It's the sky, Henry. It's the sky! It's back."

Henry's eyes finally adjusted to a daylight he had not seen in months. He looked up through the plastic sheeting to a brilliant blue swatch. Jenna had climbed off the bed and out from under the makeshift roof and was spinning like a whirling dervish, head turned to the open sky.

Already dressed, Jenna headed toward the door. "I'm goin' outside," she laughed.

"Hey, wait for me."

Henry shoved his feet inside his shoes and pulled a tee shirt over his head. He had just reached the bottom of the stairs when he heard Jenna scream. He bolted to the front door. He saw her slumped to her knees on the porch. Stretching out before her in all directions, the ground was covered in a smooth grey.

CONVERSATIONS IN SPACE[10]

The Kūaka hurtled through space, its New Hope colonists slumbering in suspended animation. Inside, all was still in the darkness except for its passengers' thoughts coalescing in a reality beyond the bounds of the conscious and subconscious.

"They say before the sixth ice age, Earth was mostly green and great oceans, lakes, and rivers were found everywhere," said Diana. "That was until super volcanos in old America, Europe and Australia erupted and filled the sky with smoke and debris."

"Before that, people lived all over the surface of Earth. They breathed fresh air and enjoyed the sun," Jacques added, "not hovelled in cubicles breathing stale air under the ice or in underground barracks."

"Do you think Boursaw 7 will be green? That there will be liquid water? Will there be air so we could live on the surface?" Connie asked.

"Projections point to an environment much like old Earth before the ice age," replied Matthew, "If not, why mount such an ambitious expedition?"

"Yes, indeed. Why mount such an expedition?" mused Jacques. "Think of it, travelling through space for nearly 500 years at near light speed. Lying in our cocoons in suspension, we hope to reach a planet that no one has ever seen, ever set foot on. In a sense, we have wagered our futures on the speculation of the scientists of Wooton Outlands Exploration."

---

[10] "Conversations In Space" appeared online in *The Worlds Within*, 11/24/2021.

"Speaking of suspension, Matthew, how is it we have this conversation?" Mario asked. "I thought nothing happened during suspension."

"Matthew, do you think we have the same conversation each time?" inquired Danyal, "or do we have different conversations? I don't remember other conversations, only what it was like before suspension."

"I don't know," Matthew replied. "They said studies had shown we might experience something like a lucid dream. Leading up to the launch, test subjects reported having such contacts during suspension, even though prior they were unknown to each other."

"How can that be?" asked Ivána, "Like Mario, I was taught suspended animation was suspension or cessation of the vital functions, with loss of consciousness. Like death, but not death."

"Yes, but perhaps our minds continue to function in a state beyond the subconscious," added Danyal. "As I understand it, our bodies continue to function, we even age, but at an extraordinarily slow rate. If we have been having the same conversation, for how long?"

"I can't remember other conversations. Doesn't mean they don't occur," said Binta.

"You're the expedition leader aren't you Matthew? Don't you know?" asked Ivána."

"Yes, I am the expedition leader, but sadly, I don't know the answer to that question. Would that I had such insight. We know our journey to Boursaw 7 will take just under 500 years at near light speed. Yet, I have no sense of the passage of time. Have any of you?"

"No."

"Not me."

"Nor I."

"I think," continued Matthew, "these conversations or dreams, if you will, exist in the moment without us remembering. What matter is there if it is the same or different each time…"

* * *

Electrical stimulation pulsed through Matthew's body. A warning signal melted his conversation. Gradually, his cocoon illuminated, allowing his eyes to accommodate to the light. He fought off the momentary nausea that accompanied coming out of suspension. His cocoon's curved lid slid open.

He breathed in the stellar convoy's stale air as illumination lights began to glow. He sat up, looking into the vast interior of the spaceship, Kūaka, filled with nine hundred and seven cocoons just like his: The New Hope Colony. Behind the Kūaka, five cargo vessels would be following, carrying everything he and his nine hundred and six companions would need to colonize Boursaw 7. Everything, perhaps, except hard work and some luck.

He ran his hand down the inside of the cocoon and retrieved a bottle. He took a sip of the liquid it contained, a syrupy elixir designed to replenish his natural saliva and provide a boost of energy. The warning signal continued to sound as he allowed his equilibrium to stabilize. He clipped the bottle to his belt, then pushed up with his arms, floating free a few inches above the cocoon. He nudged himself toward an opening in the bulkhead to the cockpit. Floating through, he pulled himself into the pilot's seat. After fastening the seat belt, he examined the ship's status hologram. Systems were operating at optimum levels. Further examination revealed the ship was receiving a hailing signal.

What? How can there be a hailing signal in unexplored space? Must be a rogue signal.

"Evaluate signal," rasped Matthew. He took another sip.

"Signal operating on standard hailing frequency."

"Open frequency to receive hailing signal." *How can this be?*

"Frequency opened," replied Kūaka's sim-voice.

"...do you receive?" floated another sim-voice over the speakers. "Unidentified vessel, this is the Elgan, identify and please state your intentions. Over..."

Matthew searched the status screen to determine the Elgan's location. It lay dead ahead, though at a considerable distance. It appeared to be matching the Kūaka's speed. "This is the stellar transport Kūaka on a peaceful mission to Boursaw 7. I am expedition leader Matthew Ellis."

"What is the purpose of your mission?"

"We are the New Hope Colony out of Earth. Our mission is to colonize Boursaw 7. What is your mission?"

There was silence.

"Come in Elgan. Repeat. This is the stellar transport Kūaka on a peaceful mission to Boursaw 7. What is your mission?"

"Kūaka reported lost 452 OES years ago."

"OES?"

"Old Earth Standard."

"I don't understand," said Matthew.

"Kūaka reported lost 452 OES years ago. Five years after launch."

"Lost? How can that be? Here we are..." Matthew scanned the status hologram, "and ship's computer confirms the Kūaka is right on course for Boursaw 7. Elgan, who are you and what is your purpose?"

74

"We are a fleet ship of the Boursawnian Space Force on routine patrol. We decided to investigate after we detected your ship approaching."

What! "Boursawnian Space Force!" stammered Matthew. "I don't understand."

"Boursaw 7 was colonized 446 OES years ago. The entire planet was incorporated as a single independent political entity named Boursawnia 50 OES years later."

"Colonized by whom?" asked Matthew.

"Emigrees from Earth under the auspices of Wooton Outlands Exploration."

"How could that be?"

"Examination of Earth records indicates that Wooton Outlands Exploration developed HLT capability soon after the Kūaka embarked on its journey."

What's that? "HLT?"

"Hyperlight Transit, the ability to travel faster than the speed of light. Old Earth news sources from the time reported allegations that The New Hope Colony project was used by Wooton Outlands Exploration as a method to secure funding from the International Off World Colonization Consortium for its own research. That company was responsible for construction of your personnel carrier and the accompanying five cargo ships. There were claims of vast overbilling which was diverted for research on the HLT technology."

"How could that be?" Matthew gripped the edge of his seat with one hand, rubbing his eyes with the other.

"According to the records, several international investigations were conducted, and an international tribunal was convened."

"What happened?"

"Ultimately, nothing. No substantial evidence could be produced. News sources cite considerable conflict and infighting among the members of the international consortium which further mired the investigation and prosecution. In the end, it resulted in little more than name calling. Wooton Outlands Exploration prevailed and eventually applied for and received an international patent for HLT. After the international consortium broke ties with Wooton Outlands Corporation, the company proceeded with its own colonization project."

Matthew took another sip from the bottle. *Wish this was something stronger.* He examined the status hologram: 6.73 years remained until the Kūaka reached Boursaw 7. "Who in authority can I speak with to make arrangements for when we reach Boursaw 7?"

After a few moments of silence, the sim-voice said, "Your inquiries will be transmitted to the appropriate Boursawnian officials. Proceed."

"What will be the procedure when we reach Boursaw 7?"

"Please clarify."

"What will we need to do so we can land?"

"It is your wish to land on Boursaw 7?"

"Of course. That's what our expedition is all about."

"Requesting answer to your question. Will hail after answer received."

"How long do you anticipate that will take?" Matthew asked.

"Unknown, as the matter will have to be addressed by the CEO and the Board of Directors. It may take several of your OES days."

"CEO and Board of Directors. I thought you said Boursawnia was an independent political entity."

76

"Radio transmission terminated," said the ship's sim-voice.

Matthew took another sip from his bottle. "Wake me when a hailing signal is received." He unfastened the seatbelt and pushed himself through the bulkhead opening. His momentum carried him down the center of the cylindrical truss system holding the cocoons of his fellow colonists. *It looks the same as the day we departed.* At the rear bulkhead, he looked through an observation port at the ship's engines and mechanicals. *All in order.* He did a half somersault and gently pushed away from the bulkhead with his feet.

He floated the length of the spaceship, mind racing. Grabbing the edge of his open cocoon to stop his momentum, he slid back inside. "Put me back in suspension until the Elgan hails us again," he said. The lid closed.

* * *

"I can't wait to plant a garden," said Vera, "in fresh air – in real soil. Hydroponics are fine, but I want to work the soil with my own hands."

"I'm going to build a house by a stream," said Jeremy, "I've photographs of my great great great grandfather's house. It was by a stream. It looks so beautiful."

"Well, I suspect we'll be busy enough for quite some time just establishing the New Hope base before we get around to planting gardens and building our dream homes," said Ibrahim. "What say you, Matthew?"

Best not say anything about what has happened until all the facts are known. "Ibrahim has a point. There will be much to do before …"

* * *

Electrical stimulation again pulsed through Matthew's body, dissolving his conversation. He swallowed back the momentary nausea as his cocoon's curved lid slid open.

"Hailing signal from the Elgan," said the ship's sim-voice.

Matthew took a sip from his bottle. "How long since the last transmission?"

"Seven days."

Seven days. I wonder why so long. "Let me get to the cockpit, then open frequency." He shoved off from his cocoon and was soon in the pilot's seat. "Open frequency."

"...Elgan. Please respond. Kūaka, this is the Elgan. Please respond."

"We receive you Elgan. This is the Kūaka," answered Matthew.

"Are we speaking with expedition leader, Matthew Ellis?"

"Yes. Were you able to get us an answer?"

"This is Marden Schnuck; I am the duly authorized representative of the CEO and Board of Directors of Boursawnia."

"Pleased to make your acquaintance, Mr. Schnuck. What information do you have for us?"

"The CEO and Board of Directors will allow members of your expedition to land on Boursawnia with certain conditions."

"Wonderful. What are the conditions?"

"I believe some background explanation is needed before we address the conditions."

"Okay."

"Technology 457 OES years ago when they assessed Boursaw 7's environment was primitive by current standards. In actuality, the environment on Boursaw 7 is quite harsh. Most of our planet is quite arid and hot, with average temperature of 325 Kelvin. Consequently, about 95% of the planet is classified as uninhabitable. Extensive mining operations are conducted in these areas. There are narrow bands of habitable land near the poles. All the mines as well as habitable land is owned and managed by Wooton Outlands Exploration."

"Where does that leave us?"

"The CEO and Board of Directors will find employment for members of your expedition at various mining operations. They, of course, will be compensated in like manner with citizens of Boursawnia and have access to housing in the standard underground dormitories rented to mine employees."

"What about the habitable lands. Is there room for us there?" asked Matthew.

"Positions in the habitable zones are made available by seniority."

"I see."

"There is another stipulation."

"What's that?"

"The expedition will have to surrender the five cargo vessels and all their contents, as well as the Kūaka, once vacated."

"But that pretty much leaves us with nothing."

"You will have employment and a place to live."

"This is a lot to consider. How much time do we have before we must make a decision?

"The Kūaka will not reach Boursaw 7 for another 6.73 Old Earth Standard years. You have some time. But be aware that political circumstances are always subject to change and opportunities may not last indefinitely."

"I understand but give me a little time and I will let you know what the decision is."

"Of course."

"Radio transmission terminated," said the ship's sim-voice.

Matthew pushed out of the pilot's seat, stopping at the opening. *What am I to do?* He looked down the rows of cocoons, then pushed forward ever so lightly, drifting down the long corridor. *They are all here. Sharing their dreams, bursting with hope and expectation of a new life. How can I face them?* He read the colonists' names on the cocoons as he floated past. He knew them all. *Do I risk going back in suspension? Will they perceive something is wrong? How do I tell them Boursaw 7 holds an existence little better than the one we fled? I can't bear the burden of destroying their dreams. Yet, holding this secret within while being with them is equally overwhelming. Perhaps it would have been better if we truly had been lost, left to float forever within our dreams.*

* * *

"Are all instructions logged and ready for implementation?" asked Matthew.

"Affirmative," Kūaka's sim-voice responded.

"Open hailing frequency to the Elgan."

"Frequency opened."

"Elgan, this is the Kūaka," said Matthew. "Do you receive?"

"Kūaka, we receive you," replied the Elgan's sim-voice.

"I have come to a decision. Is Marden Schnuck there?"

There followed a moment of silence. "This is Marden Schnuck. Proceed."

"There will be one to relocate to Boursawnia."

"Who might that be?"

"Me," whispered Matthew.

"And the rest?" inquired Schnuck.

"Kūaka's course has been reprogrammed. They will continue to follow their dreams."

DOING MRS. JOHNSON'S HAIR[11]

"Oh my! Must have dozed off." stammered Ermadine Johnson.

"You've had a nice wash, Mrs. Johnson. Everything is all clean and fresh." The unfamiliar male voice surprised her. "Now just relax while I fix your hair. Take a nap if you like. I'll be done soon."

"Just who are you and where is LaWanda?" she barked out at the young man in the grey smock. "Everyone knows she's the only one I let do my hair."

"I'm Jerome," he said, massaging her head with supple fingers. "Did I forget to mention that LaWanda wasn't available on such short notice? Now relax."

Ermadine drifted off.

* * *

The cool water on her scalp brought her back.

"… so your daughter, Rita, brought you here. I assure you, we come highly recommended. Now, just a quick rinse to get the soap out," said Jerome.

"I'm confused. Rita brought me here? Where is here?" asked Ermadine.

"You are at Rose's."

"I go to Bei Capelli," Ermadine huffed. "LaWanda has been doing my hair for years. Do you know how long it took me to find someone who could do my hair properly? And now you've washed out my perm. I just had it done. Why would you do such a thing?"

[11] "Doing Mrs. Johnson's Hair" appeared online in *Mental Papercuts*, 5/15/1019.

"I always start with a thorough wash. It gets you all clean and soft. That way I can work my magic." He let her hair sift through his fingers while he gently waved the blower back and forth. "I don't know why you let LaWanda give you a blue rinse, your hair is such a lovely white without it."

"Somebody told me it looked yellow, so I asked LaWanda to fix it. She said the blue rinse was the trick."

"Well, I can do it if you like, but your natural shade of white is much more attractive."

"Leave it then. To be honest, I never did like the blue tint all that much, anyhow."

"Excellent," cooed Jerome. "This won't take long." He picked up a round brush and began to gently work her hair. "I used some conditioner to give you more volume," he said. "It has just a hint of lavender, soft as a kitten's purr. Now we'll brush out the bangs, then mist lightly with a flexible hold hairspray to set the style and you'll be done."

"LaWanda always had me sit under the dryer."

"Oh no, Mrs. Johnson. First of all, I'm not LaWanda and second, there's no sitting under a dryer here at Rose's. Now relax."

* * *

Something soft brushed Ermadine's cheek. "Oh my, did I nod off again?" she asked. "That's not like me at all." Again, something brushed her cheek. "What are you doing?"

"Putting on the finishing touches. Just some blush."

"Makeup!" Ermadine huffed. "I don't like anyone to do my makeup for me - not even LaWanda. I'm certainly not of a mind to let a stranger do it."

"Am I still a stranger after all we've been through? Now, Mrs. Johnson, I couldn't let you leave without a little color in your cheeks, could I? At Rose's, all our clients get the full treatment. Don't worry, I won't go overboard like some people. Trust me, it will be very subtle. I like to emphasize your natural skin tones. Some color in your cheeks will compliment this lovely necklace," he said, gently touching the string of plump pearls.

"My Aunt Lilly left them to me when she died," Ermadine said. "There was a pair of matching earrings and a bracelet too."

"They're all here," said Jerome.

"But... I don't understand... I gave them to Rita years ago."

"Yes, she told me. But, she thought they would go well with your navy jacket dress and I must agree," Jerome said, straightening the collar on the jacket. "Rita said she wanted to see you wear them again."

"She did?"

"Yes, she did. Now, don't you agree it was a good thing I washed your hair? You couldn't have worn this lovely dress with that old blue rinse in your hair. Whoever did it last left it in too long and it was a bit on the purple side. They would have clashed."

Ermadine was silent for a moment. Then she whispered, "I haven't worn this dress since Fred died."

"That's what Rita told me," Jerome said softly. He paused before continuing. "I removed the old polish from your nails but I didn't put any back on. All they needed was a light buff."

"Thank you. Oh, what about my shoes?" Ermadine asked.

"The white open toed with the gold buckles were the ones Rita brought along."

"Perfect."

"Let's see, that about does it. Hair, nails, makeup, jewelry, dress and shoes. Have I forgotten anything?"

"I don't think so."

"Then my work here is done." Jerome smiled. "It's been a pleasure, Mrs. Johnson."

"Thank you Jerome. LaWanda may be out of a job."

"Yes, I am afraid so. Are you ready to go?" he asked. "Rita will be here soon."

Ermadine paused. "I don't know. Am I ready to go?" There was a knock on the door.

"I believe you are, Mrs. Johnson."

"Well, if you say so, I must be. Goodbye, Jerome."

"Goodbye, Mrs. Johnson. Say 'Hi' for me."

"Say 'Hi'? To whom?"

Before he could answer, a tall, balding man in a black suit stuck his head in the door. "Jerome, what's taking so long?" he asked. "The family will be here for their private viewing in less than fifteen minutes."

"As I've told you before, Mr. Rose," Jerome answered, closing the casket lid, "sometimes the dead need to talk a little before they go."

DO YOU KNOW WHY YOU ARE HERE TODAY?[12]

Henry watched the elevator door retract. He eyed the empty compartment before stepping in and gently pressing the button to take him to the fourth floor. There was hardly any vibration as the elevator slowly floated upward. It came to a smooth stop, and the door opened onto a beige foyer containing three doors: one to the left and two straight ahead. To the right, a long hall stretched out. A lone Looking Person was standing next to a black placard engraved with a simple "404" and an arrow which pointed to a frosted glass door at its end. Henry retrieved the appointment card from his pocket, confirming that was the door he sought.

There was nothing on the door to signify he was in the right place, so he pulled it open and walked in. Like an old movie theater ticket booth, the receptionist's cubicle protruded into the waiting room. There were two doors on either side of the receptionist, numbered one through four. A Looking Person stood behind her while three others stood around the room.

"Henry Kenkel," he said, handing the appointment card over to the receptionist. She took it and typed something on her keyboard.

"Very good, Mr. Kenkel. We were expecting you. If you would be so good as to have a seat in Room 4, we will begin. For your privacy, please make sure the door is closed securely once you have entered."

---

[12] "Do You Know Why You Are Here Today?" appeared in *pacific REVIEW - Hallucination*, 2019.

Henry walked to the door marked "4" and pushed through. The room contained two overstuffed chairs, three Looking People and a door on the opposite wall. A frumpy middle aged woman in a white smock occupied one of the chairs. He plopped down in the other. She shuffled papers from a folder she opened on her lap. Her thick glasses made her look bug eyed.

After a while she finally said, "Mr. Kenkel, my name is Dr. Beatrix Hokes. Do you prefer to be called Mr. Kenkel or may I call you Henry?"

"Henry will be fine."

"Very good, Henry. Before we start, are you currently taking any medication?"

"No."

"Do you use any recreational drugs?"

"No."

"Have you consumed any alcoholic beverages before coming in today?"

"Dr. Hokes, it's 9:00 AM."

"I am aware of that, but I have these preliminary questions I must ask. Please answer the question."

"NO!"

"No, you won't answer, or no you haven't?"

"No, I haven't."

"Thank you, Henry. Do you know why you are here today?"

"My brother has petitioned the court to have me undergo a psychiatric evaluation to determine my competency to serve as executor of our mother's estate."

"And have you formed an opinion as to why he would choose that course of action?" she asked.

"The kind thing would be to say he was concerned about my wellbeing. In reality, my brother is most accurately described as a ne'er do well, given to drink and recreational drug use. He has never been one to hold a steady job, either. Consequently, his wife left him and took their child. Mother was afraid my brother would squander any money she left him and leave her grandchild wanting for proper care. As a result, she established a trust for her grandchild and designated me as the administrator. My brother vehemently resents the arrangement and wants to get his hands on that money. If he can prove I am not competent, then he stands to break the trust."

Dr. Hokes closed the folder and stared intently at Henry. "And how does that make you feel?"

"Angry? Sad?" Henry replied. "I guess a little of both. Regardless, I am a private individual and I do resent this prying."

"Then why not dole out enough money to keep your brother happy until it's gone and be done with it?"

"That's not what my mother wanted. I have a responsibility to honor her wishes. Besides, as a CPA, I would consider allowing my brother to recklessly dissipate the Trust's assets as tantamount to misfeasance on my part."

"Let's move on. Your brother claims in his deposition that you are agoraphobic, barely able to function in public. What have you to say about that?"

"I would say my presence here today would dispel that notion," Henry answered.

"He goes on to claim that you live at a soup kitchen."

"I would say his lawyer has quite an ambitious imagination. More likely, my brother has grossly misrepresented the situation," said Henry. "I live in a three story building which, I might add, I own. My apartment is on the top floor. I maintain a walk up office on the second floor for my CPA business. The ground floor is leased for a dollar a year to a nonprofit, pay-what-you-can community restaurant. There, folks have the option to either pay the recommended price, which helps pay for a meal forward for the next person, pay what they can, or volunteer for 30 minutes in exchange for a meal."

"Of course," said Dr. Hokes, "none of this, even if true, would be sufficient to prove you are not competent to serve as trust administrator or the executor of your mother's estate. However, the petition contains other assertions which may prove more problematic to address. Your brother claims you installed a toilet in your coat closet."

"Hardly," said Henry. "I had a toilet room installed within my regular bathroom. It is a feature growing in popularity and considered in some circles as a luxury."

"I see. The petition goes on to say that you sleep in a cold locker of the type used in a morgue to store bodies," continued Dr. Hokes. "Is that true?"

"I have a custom-made sleeping compartment which employs a roll out mechanism of the type used in morgues," Henry answered. "The design is based on the popular Japanese capsule hotels. I have customized mine with a television, electronic console, and wireless internet connection. At the push of a button, the door slides open and my bed rolls out. Push another and it rolls back in and the door closes. I also have an app on my phone which can do the same thing. Quite cozy and comfy." Henry paused a moment before continuing. "Dr. Hokes, I don't think I'm here because of my choice of bedroom design."

"Of course not. I believe all this is just window dressing tossed in by your brother's lawyer to lay a foundation to support the real issue. The petition claims you experience hallucinations and have since you were a child."

"Hallucinations are defined as an experience involving the apparent perception of something not present. I've never seen anything that wasn't present," asserted Henry.

"It is a serious allegation," Dr. Hokes said patiently, "not to be taken lightly. These other accusations, as you have easily proved unfounded, are there to support this accusation. In his deposition, he says you have admitted seeing imaginary people."

"Suppose I deny the accusation. Then, it becomes a matter of my word against his."

"His lawyer has brought forth a deposition from one Ardalene Weldt. Are you acquainted with her?"

"We dated," Henry said curtly.

"She claims you admitted the same to her. Any truth in her statement?" asked Dr. Hokes.

Henry sat silent for a few seconds before muttering, "How'd that bastard find her?"

"What was that?"

"Oh nothing. I had not considered he might seek her out."

"So, there is something here?"

"As I mentioned, I dated Ardalene for a while. In fact, I grew quite serious about her. She worked for one of my clients. He distrusted the internet, so he had Ardalene deliver copies of his financial records every month for me to review. One day, she asked if the food downstairs was good. I told her it was and offered to buy her lunch. What started as a casual business encounter grew into a friendship and eventually a romance - at least on my part."

"What happened?" asked Dr. Hokes.

"I was ready for a long term commitment, but I knew for it to work, I couldn't keep the Looking People a secret from her."

"The Looking People? Who are they and what did they have to do with Ardalene?"

"They are the hallucinations my brother is talking about," said Henry. "Except they are not hallucinations. They are real."

"Then why would he call them hallucinations?" asked Dr. Hokes.

"Because I am the only one I know of who can see the Looking People."

"Surely, Henry, you can see how people might call that a hallucination. Tell me, what do these Looking People do? Do they talk to you? Do they tell you to do things?"

"Oh, nothing like that. They just gaze at things."

"Do they gaze at you?"

"Sometimes."

"How does that feel?"

"I am used to it, although there are sometimes I find them intrusive."

"When was the last time you saw one of these Looking People?"

"Let's see. There was one in the hall, four in the waiting room, counting the one standing behind the receptionist. Then, there are three in here with us."

Dr. Hokes looked around the tiny room. "You must forgive me, Henry, apparently I am one of those who can't see the Looking People. Tell me, who or what are they looking at?"

"Two are looking at me and the other is focused on you."

"I see how that might be intrusive, if I could see them, of course. How many Looking People do you think there are?

"Too many to count," said Henry.

"Where do you encounter them?"

"With few exceptions, they're everywhere."

"And those exceptions?"

"You won't find them in any place only big enough for one person, like a phone booth or a lavatory on an airplane."

"Do they follow you around?" asked Dr. Hokes

"No, they never move, but I never see the same one twice. It's like they wait until I am not around to move. One fact remains, though; no matter where I go, Looking People will be there."

"What do they look like?"

"Like regular people," said Henry

"So if you go to the mall, are Looking People there?"

"Yes."

"How do you tell them apart from regular people?"

"Looking People never blink their eyes. They never move."

"If it's crowded and they can't be seen, don't regular people bump into them on occasion?" asked Dr. Hokes.

"Have you ever cracked an egg into a bowl to make scrambled eggs," asked Henry, "and noticed a bit of shell down in the raw egg white?"

"Sure."

"And did you try to trap it on the side of the bowl with your finger, only to find it shift to one side or another? Then, when you pulled your finger out, it slid back to its original position. That's what happens."

"When did you first distinguish Looking People from real people?"

"Looking People are real," Henry sighed. "When did you first distinguish birds from leaves, or trees from telephone poles? Looking People have been part of my world since I can remember.

They have always been there. Of course, as soon as I could talk, I told my parents about the Looking People. They took me to the doctor. He told my parents my Looking People were nothing more than imaginary friends and not to worry. Later, my classmates in school ridiculed me for talking about the Looking People, so I learned to keep quiet."

"I want to go back to your statement about Ardalene," said Dr. Hokes. "Despite the issues you mention, you decided to tell Ardalene about the Looking People?"

"It's easy to keep them a secret from casual acquaintances and clients," Henry started, "but not so when one enters into a serious relationship. Know why I have my toilet in a closet and I sleep in a capsule? It's because I need some privacy. Even though I have lived with Looking People watching me all my life, I still don't relish them watching me take a dump. Likewise, I am uneasy with the thought of them watching me while I sleep."

"Hence, your toilet closet and sleeping compartment."

"Exactly," said Henry, "so when the time came to take the next step with Ardalene, I wasn't willing to share our physical intimacy with the Looking People."

"Couldn't you turn out the lights?"

"I would know they were still there, watching. Could you make love to your partner in a dark room with someone standing next to your bed?"

"Not my first choice," conceded Dr. Hokes.

"Precisely. I knew I couldn't ask her to share my sleeping compartment without explaining why I couldn't share her bed. Needless to say, she freaked and no matter how much I tried to convince her, she couldn't accept my explanation and that was the end of our love affair. I never thought she would use this against me, though."

"Well, I am sorry," soothed Dr. Hokes, "but you will have to admit, the whole premise is hard to believe. You still haven't offered any proof that these Looking People are real. I'm afraid your brother has a fairly compelling argument."

"Do you believe in God?" asked Henry. "I believe most people do. I know I do. Now to my knowledge, the only proof of God's existence is the purported writings of a few of his disciples who lived over 2000 years ago. As far as I know, no one alive at this moment has seen God. No one has ever taken a picture of God, never found his fingerprints on anything, yet millions of people believe in His existence. And what about Sasquatch, aliens, or ghosts? Lots of people believe in them. Some even have a few blurry pictures to back up their claims, but when it comes down to it, nobody has any real proof. Does that mean all these people are hallucinating, they lack the competency to make decisions about their lives?"

"Well no," Dr. Hokes replied.

"Dr. Hokes am I real?" asked Henry.

"Of course, I see you sitting across from me."

"So, I'm real because you see me. Correct?"

"And hear you," added Dr. Hokes.

"What if I was mute? Would I still be real?"

"Of course. I suppose I could always reach out and touch you to confirm it."

"What if I was on the other side of a busy street? Would I be real?" asked Henry.

"Yes, I could still see you."

"If there is a blind person standing there who can't see me, am I still real?"

"Don't be ridiculous," chided Dr. Hokes.

"Even if they couldn't see or hear me?"

"I would verify that you are real."

"I see. Are you real, Dr. Hokes?"

"Of course," she huffed, "you see me sitting here, don't you?"

"Yes, of course, but we must remember I also see Looking People. Perhaps I might blink and . . . 'Voilà!' you would disappear."

Dr. Hokes wrinkled her brow. "I don't think this thread of discussion is contributing much to your evaluation at this point."

"I agree Dr. Hokes, so let's cut to the chase. I believe in God. I'm a law abiding citizen. I maintain a robust CPA practice. I give back to my community. The fact that I happen to see Looking People, doesn't affect my ability to get along in society or make sound judgements. Based on this, I can't see why my competency is in question. I appreciate you have your role in all this. In no small measure, I am sure, it will help me in disproving my brother's allegations."

Dr. Hokes looked at Henry for some time before speaking. "Henry, you make a strong argument. I see no reason why you should be removed as executor of your mother's estate or administrator of the trust."

"Thanks, Dr. Hokes." Henry heard a knock on the door behind her. He looked up just in time to see a tall balding man wearing jeans and a cardigan sweater step through the door. He had a file folder in his hand.

The man sat down in the chair opposite Henry. After a while he said, "Mr. Kenkel, Sorry to keep you waiting all alone in here. My name is Dr. Rheel. Do you prefer to be called Mr. Kenkel or may I call you Henry?"

"Henry will be fine."

"Very good, Henry. Do you know why you are here today?"

BLACK ROLLERS[13]

Morglan felt the fine grit on his teeth as he sucked the inside of his mouth for some saliva to swallow. A violent gust from the dust storm, now in its second year, had swept him out of his carrier. He watched its dim shape melt away. *The black rollers. That's what they called the storms of the Dust Bowl in old America 200 years ago.*

His thoughts drifted back over the span of ten orbits around V335 Aquilae, what the exo-dreamers had dubbed Sagan's Star. *How had it come to this?* They had traveled across the universe to establish the first colony on Sagan 5. It was not the idyllic Earth-type world all had hoped to find, but by the time their expedition blasted off, neither was Earth. The 6th Ice Age was peaking. The Yellowstone super volcano in old America had erupted, throwing plate-tectonic movement into chaos. The resultant changes in ocean and atmosphere circulation patterns resulted in a dramatic and devastating drop in temperature. In comparison to the icy world Earth had become, Sagan 5 was a paradise.

* * *

Linden stood on the ridge of the command hut roof, clinging to a long dead antenna against the force of the storm. She and it struggled to remain upright. The devastation had accelerated at an alarming rate, catching them unprepared. The others had already left. Lindon had stayed at the command hut to coordinate the evacuation. While that was in progress, she had assigned Bosch and Pérez to search for Morglan.

---

[13] "Black Rollers" appeared online in *The Free Bundle*, 11/2019.

Linden strained to make out the approaching carrier. Seeing them, she pulled up the mantle of her envirohood, and yelled, "Any sign of Morglan?"

"No, ma'am," shouted Pérez in return, as he steered the carrier toward the blurry figure.

"We'll never find him. Can't see a damn thing in all this mess," added Bosch.

"Have you looked everywhere?" yelled Linden.

"Yeah," barked Bosch looking at Pérez for support. His companion nodded.

"Around the greenhouse?" asked Linden.

"No way the old man could have gotten that far," said Pérez.

"So you lazy bastards haven't looked everywhere," spat Linden. "Turn that thing around and go check it out."

"Come on Cap," whined Bosch, "ain't no way he made it that far. Besides, everyone else has gone. It's time we made tracks before we get swallowed up."

"West, about two klicks," she yelled, pointing to her left. "Go!"

* * *

Morglan drew a ragged breath, lungs gurgling. *How were we to know? How was I to know? I was expedition leader, I am responsible, but how were we to know?*

For seven years, the colony had thrived on Sagan 5, building their dwellings from bits and pieces of lander craft, native stone and mud. They scratched a subsistence life from the narrow band of semi-arid land that girded the planet's equator. Virtually all of the planet's water was contained in its frozen polar caps or the deep aquifers that flowed beneath the surface. Some exoplanet scientists speculated that Sagan 5 had once been totally

100

covered in water. That was before some primordial event resulted in a cataclysmic environmental change.

At first, the colonists made long journeys from the narrow band of arable land around Sagan 5's equator to retrieve ice, which they stored in holding ponds, using the melt to irrigate their fields. Later, they dug wells from which to draw water.

Every muscle in Morglan's body screamed for oxygen. His legs, refusing to cooperate, were little more than aching dead weight. The ferocity of the storm crushed him. Almost blinded by its fury, he searched for shelter with his hands as he pulled himself along. *The Okies headed west to escape... If I could only rest for a few moments...*

* * *

Pérez checked his compass as he struggled to keep on a heading toward the greenhouse. The storm seemed intent on sweeping them into oblivion. He corrected course, hunkering down against the storm surge. He leaned close to Bosch.

"Why'd the old fool have to go wander off just when we were getting ready leave?" he rasped.

"I think this godforsaken storm drove him nuts. It'll do the same to all of us if it don't kill us first. Hell, we may already be nuts. This storm has been going on for two years. Who knows? We might even be dead and never realize it in all this mess," Bosch growled. He wiped his visor and stared into the roiling storm.

"See anything?" asked Pérez, keeping his eyes glued to the compass.

Bosch stared ahead. Suddenly, a shape materialized directly in their path. "Watch out!" he cried.

Pérez looked up from his compass just in time to avoid ramming the empty carrier and coasted to a stop. He maneuvered as close to it as the storm would allow, without risking a collision. "Looks empty," he said.

"Yeah, can we go back now?" pleaded Bosch.

"No. Cap'll have our hides. We'll check this out, then head for the greenhouse." Pérez peered into the murk. "By my reckoning, it's only a few hundred yards further. There's always a chance he made it there."

"Do you think Cap is right?" asked Bosch.

"About Morglan? I think he's dead and the likelihood of finding him is pretty small."

"No, about waiting out the storm on the polar caps."

* * *

Morglan's left hand touched the edge of something substantial. Pulling himself forward, he reached under with his right hand to find a small cavity. As the scud swirled in gusts, he wriggled his head and upper torso inside, leaving his legs exposed. He pulled off his hood, gasping for air.

His thoughts wandered as he struggled to remain conscious. *How were we to know?* In year eight, Sagan 5 began to wobble on its axis. Slightly at first, the wobble continued to increase in degree of tilt. By the end the year nine, the tilt was enough to trigger the devastating climatic changes which precipitated the onslaught of violent storms. By the end of the year ten, the storms morphed into a tempest without end.

As he struggled to breathe, the inexorable storm continued its assault.

* * *

By now, the ridge of the command hut was fully inundated. Linden strained hear the sound of the carrier over the howl of the storm. Pérez and Bosch had been gone long enough to complete their search and return. She hoped they had not died

102

or worse deserted, leaving her stranded. The com in her envirohood crackled, long rendered useless by the static electricity generated by the storm.

Finally the carrier appeared bucking against the storm caps. Bosch threw Linden a line, which she tied off on the antenna to keep it from floating away. She immediately saw the body rolling in the water on the floorboards. "Is Morglan dead?"

"Yeah," said Pérez, bailing rainwater.

"Where'd you find him?"

"You were right," said Bosch, "he was at the greenhouse. Found him stuck halfway through a roof vent. His hood was gone. Musta drowned when the water rose above the roof."

"Should we leave him here?" asked Pérez.

"No," said Lindon, climbing in. "We'll take him with us. Better get going before we get swamped. She grabbed a bucket and began bailing. "Once we find the others, we'll figure out what to do."

"He musta gone crazy," said Pérez. "What was he thinking to do such a thing, Cap?"

"I don't know," said Lindon. "Who can tell what goes through a dying man's mind?"

THE CHANGELING[14]

"Don't talk to me like I'm crazy!" Fiona barked. Her eyes flashed at her husband. "I tell you that's not Brandon."

"But honey, can't you hear what you are saying? You want me to believe the fairies have taken Brandon. If they did, who is in the nursery? He sure looks like the baby we brought home from the hospital three days ago. If you said the nurses screwed up and somehow switched our baby with another, I might find that plausible. But fairies, how do you imagine that sounds?

"Like the truth. I don't know why you won't believe me. A mother knows her baby, and that thing is not my baby."

"Fi, I don't mean to be disrespectful," David said, "but just because your Mamó is from Ireland and casts herself a neo-pagan, it doesn't mean all those fairy stories she filled your head with are true. I'm sure she convinced herself she had the facility to feel the presence of fairies. No doubt so convincing, she got you believing you could do it too. But you're a grown woman now and should realize all her malarkey was just old wives' tales. Honey, I love you and you know I support you. And that's why I must tell you you're letting your imagination run out of control. Besides I thought fairies were little bitty things. How could they carry off a baby? Why would they even do such a thing?"

"Cause they need a real baby to inject a dwindling and weak stock with a fresh, healthy human strain," Fiona shot back.

"Do you hear yourself?" asked David. "Change the boogeymen from 'fairies' to 'greys' and you have the classic alien abduction story. I got news for you, that's not real either. Fi,

[14] "The Changeling" appeared online in *CafeLit*, 6/11/2020.

you've got to stop this. Our beautiful blonde, blue eyed baby is sleeping in the nursery. He needs, I need, his mother to come back to reality."

"I never left it and I'll thank you to leave Mamó out of it. She could sense the Fae and so can I."

"If the fairies took Brandon, who is in the nursery?"

"It's called a changeling. When the Fae steal a baby, they leave a changeling in its place. This changeling can be an ugly old elf or maybe a simulacrum they fashioned of wood or clay but, under a proper spell, it appears to be an exact replica of the stolen child. Later it seems to die and is so buried while the real baby is raised by the Fae."

"Oh brother! Listen, Janie at work said that sometimes new mothers get this thing called postpartum depression. She says it really does a number on new moms. Maybe that is what's going on with you. Think maybe you should go see Dr. Winslow? Maybe she can prescribe something."

Abruptly, Fiona rose from her chair. She glared at David. "And just who are you to be discussing me with some bimbo from the office pool? You got no right to be talking behind my back. And I don't need a prescription from Dr. Winslow."

"It's not like that," David said. "Janie just asked how everything was going with the new baby and one thing led to another. She's experienced the depression thing and really had a bad time until she saw her doctor. She was only trying to offer a suggestion."

"Well, I suggest she mind her own business and not speak of that of which she has no knowledge. And as for you, I'll appreciate if you keep your big mouth shut when it comes to my affairs."

"But, they're my affairs too! However, you don't seem to be able to see that. You forget Brandon is my child also, and I would like to think I have some say in the matter."

"Then say it to me and not the office gossip!"

"It's just that I'm worried about you."

"You don't have to worry about me. I know what's real and not real. You best be worrying about that thing in the other room."

As if on cue, a wail blared from the baby monitor.

David flipped the lever on his recliner and started to stand up. "Probably needs to be changed," he said softly. "I'll go."

"Oh no, stay where you are. I'll take care of it. After all isn't that what a good mother is supposed to do?"

"I didn't say you weren't a good mother. Having your first baby can be overwhelming for anyone. I was thinking maybe I should do a little more and let you rest up."

"Shut up David. Every time you open your mouth you sink deeper in your own stupidity. Don't worry, I'm perfectly capable of taking care of the situation."

"Okay."

Fiona stood motionless while the wailing continued to flow from the baby monitor. She waited for David to sink back into his recliner before she strode out of the room into the kitchen.

The wailing continued as David picked up the controller for the baby monitor to view the nursery on its LED screen. He could see Brandon's tiny arms and legs twitching as he cried. Fiona appeared. Reaching the crib, she raised a fist above her head. Before he could make out what she was holding, she swung her arm down toward Brandon.

The wailing stopped.

David jumped up from his recliner and tore down the hall. He lurched into the nursery. "Fiona! What have you done?" he screamed, shoving Fiona aside. He peered into Brandon's crib. The chef's knife Fiona had brought from the kitchen protruded from the infant's torso. David gasped in anguish as a crimson Rorschach blotch wicked out into the sheets. In the next moment, the bloody stain evaporated, and the lifeless body melted into a lump of clay resembling a clumsily formed gingerbread man.

Fiona smiled. "Don't worry, David" she said, "I killed the changeling. Now all we have to do is find Brandon."

CRINA

Such a long time had passed. Crina watched the people gather. *So many have come and gone. There is Marku, leading his small group.*

Waving his bright red walking stick above his head, Marku called out, "This way everyone, this way." He stopped, allowing his group to gather around him. "Once again, I am Marku, your guide to Grondo, the great castle of King Brută de Fier, the Iron Brute. He was so called because in 1375, he thwarted the attempt by the Golden Horde to take over his country. In the time of Brută, his kingdom was called Ruthenia, a name now long forgotten."

***

"Let me see your teeth," said Necula, grabbing the young girl's face with his spindly fingers. He turned her head toward the flickering candlelight.

"Her teeth are perfect," said Alin, her father.

Necula held up his free hand, "I shall be the judge of that. King Brută is very particular about these things. As the Vrăjitor, it would be my head if she displeased his eye."

"I assure you, everything about her appearance is perfect," said Alin. "There are other aspects that may come to question."

"And those are?"

"As I said, she is perfect in appearance. However, she does not speak. Never has she spoken a single word."

"That is of little consequence. The King does not seek a curtezană for pleasant conversation. A flawless countenance and soft pliant flesh is what he seeks."

"There is one other thing."

"And what is that?" asked Necula. "I grow tired of all this talk."

"Since she was born, she has never shed a tear."

"You think the King is interested in the silly emotions of peasant girls? It is of no significance. Still, I will see her teeth or the deal is off."

"As you command," said Alin. "Crina, open your mouth."

***

That was how it had started. Crina turned her attention back to Marku.

"Brută was a stern ruler," he said, "giving no quarter to his country's enemies. But to his people, he was a gentle ruler and much beloved by his subjects"

***

"You may close your mouth, child," said Necula. "You possess a rare beauty indeed. King Brută will be pleased. Your name is Crina? Such a pretty flower you are. Just what he has sought so long." Necula snapped his fingers to summon the bent old woman who had been lurking in the shadows. The pale amber light of the tallow candle made the deep creases in her cheeks look like swirling black tattoos. "Now the rest," he said.

***

If only Marku knew what really happened. Crina continued to listen as the tour guide droned on.

"The responsibility," said Marku, "of finding the very best candidates for the Court was assigned to the King's Mage and advisor, Necula. It is said that being chosen for the King's Court was a great honor and much sought after, for life at Castle Grondo was considered a grand existence. The selection process was an elaborate affair, conducted with great pomp and circumstance."

"Take that filthy tunic off," Narezza said, "so that the Vrăjitor can inspect you." Crina held tightly to her tunic. "Do you think you can serve the King in such rags, you foolish girl?" Crina stood motionless. "I said remove it!" Narezza pointed a gnarled finger at the offending garment. Crina's tunic began to burn her skin like hot coals. She immediately loosened her cinch and pulled the garment over her head, tossing it aside. She turned her head away as she tried to cover her nakedness. "No need for modesty here," said Narezza, "Now stand still for Master Necula." She slowly raised her finger. Crina reluctantly dropped her arms to her side.

Necula studied Crina's face while stroking her soft, honey colored hair. He walked behind her, leaned in close and drew a deep breath. "You indeed are special," he said, laying one hand on Crina's bare shoulder while the other caressed her hair. The odor of rotting meat and sulfur engulphed Crina. She trembled. Necula whispered in her ear, "No need to worry about me. I wouldn't dare spoil such a gift for the King." He stood back from Crina. "First, you will be bathed and anointed with the rarest of perfumed oils. That will rid you of the dirt and peasants' stench. Then, no more tattered, wool tunic. Instead, you will be dressed in the finest silk from the East and adorned with gold and sapphires from Solomon's mines. Only then will you be presented to the King." He nodded to Narezza. "Pay the man."

The woman reached into her pouch and tossed a handful of silver coins on the table. Gathering them, Alin said, "Crina, my dear, you must go with the Vrăjitor. The King has ordered it and we will be killed if we refuse. Remember, it is a great honor and privilege to serve the King." He turned his head to avoid seeing the despair in his daughter's eyes.

"Narezza, bring the girl," said Necula. He threw open the door and disappeared into the thin afternoon sunlight.

"Come child," said Narezza, picking up Crina's tunic. "Get dressed. We must be off."

"Let me get her cloak," said Alin.

"She'll have no need for a cloak," said Narezza. "We have all she needs."

"But it will be cold in the mountains."

Eyes glaring, Narezza pointed a crooked finger at Alin. At once, he winced in pain. "She'll have no need for a cloak. Besides, what do you care? You have your thirty groschen."

"Yes, I understand," said Alin.

Narezza grabbed Crina's arm, yellowed nails digging into the girl's flesh as she tried to twist away.

"You must go, Crina, my dearest daughter. Do not resist," said Alin. "After all, a deal is a deal, especially one made with the King. Remember, it is a great honor to serve him." She relaxed, allowing Narezza to lead her away.

Outside, a small horse cart awaited. Crina could see Necula riding away, whipping his black stallion furiously. Narezza pointed to the small bench at the front of the cart. "Up with you and be quick about it. We have a long journey ahead of us."

***

It never changes. Crina watched the visitors crowd around Marku, hanging on his every word.

"One can only imagine," said Marku, "the warm reception that they who were chosen to serve the King received at Castle Grondo. They would have passed through the grand gates in their horse-drawn carriages, paraded through the royal courtyard, then greeted by the Grand Steward. From there, they would be ushered

112

to sumptuous chambers to refresh and rest before meeting the King."

***

The wind was chill the next evening when Crina arrived at Castle Grondo, perched on the precipice of Mount Slonim. Strong and austere, it gleamed amber in the waning sunlight. "Come, come," said Narezza, pulling her charge from the cart. She led Crina in the shadows on a narrow path between the castle wall and the cliff's edge until they reached a small entrance. Inside, they ascended rough steps hewn from the living rock.

Crina followed Narezza as they climbed the narrow, dimly lit stairwell. The musty air stuck in Crina's throat. Every few feet, the old woman would point to a dormant candle in a rusty sconce hanging from the rock wall. She would then snap her fingers and it would burst into flame. The flickering light cast ghoulish shadows dancing on the walls. Eventually, the uneven stairs leveled out into a circular landing with many corridors leading away. Narezza led Crina through an opening to the left and down many passages until they reached a latched wooden door. Narezza drew back the bolt and pushed the door open. Inside was a large chamber filled with the light from blazing torches. A large wooden tub sat next to a roaring hearth. A thin, pale young woman with an angry scar on her cheek limped to the fireplace. She used a hook to swing the crane out. A large copper pot hung at its tip. She drew a vial from the mantle and poured its contents into the steaming water. The scent of roses filled the air.

"This is Maricara," said Narezza, "she will serve you. Once she stood where you now stand, radiant and beautiful, but she failed to fulfill the King's desires." Crina winced as she watched the frail woman struggle to heft the large copper pot from its hook and pour the steaming, scented water into the tub.

113

"Now, off with those rags and into your bath. After that, Maricara will prepare your supper. Sleep well tonight and rest, for when the sun rises, you will be summoned to the King." She turned to Maricara. "Do not dally. You still have supper to prepare for the Vrăjitor and me." Narezza left the room, pulling the door shut behind her. The sound of the latch bolt slamming home rang out. Crina raced to the door, frantically pulling at its handle. The door did not move. She tried again and again until her arms ached. Slumping against the door she looked at Maricara, pleading with her eyes for some help.

"It is no use," said Maricara. "Unless you want to suffer the same fate as me, you should do as the Vrăjitor's hag bids."

***

And so I was lost.

"Stay close now. I can't come looking for you if you get lost in the crowd," said Marku. "Now where was I? Oh yes. It is said the King always had the welfare of his servants in mind and treated them with kindness and civility. That is why his court loved him so. Now stay close." Marku raised his walking stick and moved to another location, his group shuffling behind.

***

"So you have brought me something, Vrăjitor?" asked Brută.

"Yes, Sire." Answered Necula. "A most beautiful bauble. Narezza has taken her to the chamber to be bathed and perfumed. I believe you will be most pleased. There are two things you should know, though hardly worth mentioning."

"Then why mention them? You know I have little patience for such prattle."

"Of course, Sire. According to her churl of a father, she neither speaks nor sheds a tear."

114

Brută tugged at his grey beard. "Hmmm. As you say, hardly worth mentioning. Will she be soft in my bed and look good in the Grand Hall?"

"No doubt she will be soft," answered Necula. "How cooperative she will be is something difficult to predict,"

"Ahhh. Leave that for me to find out. Sometimes a good struggle is satisfying and not screaming out in the moment would be convenient."

Necula bowed his head in acknowledgement. "As for your other concern, I can say, my King, she will be the most beautiful ever to adorn the Grand Hall."

"Above all the others?"

"Yes Sire."

"Very well, bring her to the Grand Hall first thing after breakfast."

The next morning, Maricara was combing Crina's long blond hair when Narezza entered. She brushed the maidservant aside and caressed Crina's face with leathery fingers. "See how fine her skin is. No need to hide it with powder or rouge. Now some perfume before she dons her tunic." Narezza handed Maricara a crystal vial. "A mixture of myrrh, rose, and sweet gum will please the King." Maricara removed the topper. The fragrance reminded her of a moment when she wore fine silk and the same perfume, but it had ended badly at the hands of a displeased King. She fought back her tears as she poured a few drops of the essence on her fingers and proceeded to gently rub the scented oil onto Crina's neck and shoulders. Then she removed Crina's plain woolen tunic, replacing it with a fine chemise. Over that, she placed a finely embroidered white linen tunic.

"Here child, put these on," said Narezza, holding out a pair of delicate leather slippers. "Can't have you walking around barefoot to meet the King. Hurry, he awaits."

Narezza led Crina through many hallways and passages, always climbing upward until they arrived at a spacious room. Before they entered, Narezza pulled her hood closed except for a small slit from which she could see. "The King doesn't like an old face," she said. "Don't forget to bow." She led Crina into the room. The morning light poured in through a large window. It was a pleasant contrast to the dark rooms and passageways. Necula was standing next to a swarthy man sitting in an ornately carved chair. His beard was tinged with grey. Narezza tugged Crina's arm downward to remind her to bow.

"You may rise," said Brută. "Come closer." Crina stepped forward until she stood full in the sunlight. Her honey colored hair shimmered.

"Do you not agree that she is most comely?" Necula asked.

The King stood up and approached Crina, his face inches away from hers. He smelled of stale wine and sweat. "Yes," he said, stroking her hair and allowing his rough hand to trail the length of her arm. "She may well be the one."

"Excellent," said Necula.

"With me," said Brută. He led Crina through another door. On the other side, she found herself in the apse of a very large room. "The Grand Hall of Castle Grondo," said Brută. They were standing on an elevated dais, featuring a carved throne festooned with jewels. Just behind it and to the left was a simpler, yet still elegant chair. In front, steps led down to the floor of the rectangular expanse stretching out before them. Mullioned windows ran along either side, allowing the morning sunlight to bathe the interior with a golden glow.

***

Now, more will be added to the litany of lies. Crina watched Marku lead his group to the center of the Grand Hall.

"Look about you," said Marku, waving his walking stick in a wide circle above his head. "Behold the famous statues of Grondo. Like the Catholic Stations of the Cross, there are fourteen statues situated around the Grand Hall. Renowned for their lifelike quality, many say they are unequaled in beauty. Not even the Greeks or Romans had statues to compare to these. From what stone they were carved is unknown, nor is it known who the sculptor, or sculptors, were. But, whether it be the stone, the one who carved it, or a combination of the two, all agree the statues possess an uncanny lifelike appearance. King Brută himself personally approved each before it was installed."

***

"See my statui femei," said Brută, pointing out the ornate pilasters running halfway up the walls between the windows. On all but one rested a life-sized statue of a young woman. "They are my obsession. It has taken me years to collect them. There is one yet still vacant. That one," he said, pointing to the empty pilaster on the right of the dais. "Very soon, it will house my most beautiful statui of all." Crina turned her eyes down from the sight of the nude figures, focusing on a wide silver strip in the polished marble floor. Running obliquely from one end of the space to the other, it was dotted with inlaid symbols. Near its center rested a bright spot of sunlight.

Necula stepped forward. "That is our sun calendar. It is the greatest in the world. It marks the days and significant astrological events. The golden sunburst," he said, pointing to a symbol near the empty pilaster, "marks our King's birthday. We shall have a great feast on that day"

117

***

How many times have I watched that spot of sunlight crawl along the floor? More than I care to remember. Crina watched Marku twirl his walking stick before pointing it to the floor at their feet.

"Before you stretches the magnificent sun calendar of Grondo," he said. "Installed when the castle was constructed, it is considered a marvel of astronomical engineering." He pointed toward the ceiling. "High above your heads you will see the builders of Castle Grondo placed a hole. It is strategically located so that a shaft of sunlight is projected onto the silver inlay. That strip is engraved with the days of the year and signs of the zodiac. It is said to rival the sun calendars of The Basilica of San Petronio in Bologna, Italy and the Cathedral of Our Lady of Strasbourg."

Lies and more lies. Crina listened as Marku continued.

"In 1387, Brută successfully quelled an insurrection by the Boyars, a powerful class of the nobility. It was thought they had been planning for some time to overthrow him and seize control of Ruthenia for themselves. Having defeated the rebellion, Brută held a grand feast to commemorate his victory. He invited his most trusted and loyal subjects."

***

"Today, however," said Necula, "we will have a feast to commemorate something else, a great victory for our King. Soon the servants will begin the preparations. The King has invited many special guests. As his curtezană, you will be his escort, after which, if it is the King's pleasure, you will join him in his private suite. As for now, it is time for you to return to your room to get ready. "Narezza," he called, "take her and wait for me."

Narezza led Crina back to her room, where she instructed Maricara to prepare her for the celebration. Maricara combed out

118

Crina's hair and rubbed more perfume onto her neck and shoulders. Then they waited.

After some time, Narezza appeared. "Here is her gown," she said, handing over the garment. "Dress her and be quick about it."

Maricara removed Crina's linen tunic, which she replaced with a delicate white silk gown. It was embroidered with gold thread.

Narezza reached into her cloak and held out a sapphire necklace and matching circlet. "Here, put these on her and take those leather slippers off her feet. Get the satin ones with the garnets and pearls from the wardrobe. Can't have her walking around in leather while wearing silk and sapphires. Hurry, the King awaits."

After Crina had been dressed, Narezza led her back to the Grand Hall. Crina sat next to Brută on the dais while the Boyar noblemen, accompanied by their wives or consorts, filtered in. Each was announced by a page who led them before the dais, where they bowed before the King. Then, they were escorted to their appointed place at the grand table. It was piled high with roasted meats and other delicacies. Flagons of spiced wine dotted the table. After all the guests had arrived, Brută arose, taking Crina's hand, and walked down the steps to the head of the table. He surveyed the assembly before nodding. At that simple gesture, the chamberlain blew a horn, signaling for everyone to be seated. The guests proceeded to wash their hands in the bowls of water at their places. Once finished, retainers removed the bowls, replacing them with silver plates. All eyes rested on Brută.

He stood up, extending an empty crystal goblet to his guests. "I offer you a toast." He turned the goblet over. "Laşi, trădători!" he shouted. "Yes, to you cowards and traitors I offer an empty cup. I know you plan to betray me, that you desire to seize my throne." He smashed the goblet on the floor. "Before this evening is through, I'll fill my cup with your blood." A collective gasp filled the air. Then, he drew his knife and slashed the throat of the nearest Boyar. His soldiers, who were masquerading as retainers, drew their knives and joined in the slaughter. In a matter of minutes, Brută's guests were dead, their blood staining the polished marble floor.

Brută returned to his seat next to Crina. Flecks of blood stained her cheek and silk gown. He tore off a chunk of roast venison with a bloody hand and took a large bite. "I'm hungry, are you?" he asked. "I never feel so alive as when I have killed an enemy." Crina ran from the table, running up the steps to the dais into the waiting grasp of Necula. He thrust her toward Narezza, who blew some powder in her face. "That should slow you down," she said, as Crina continued to struggle. "It is useless," Necula said. Crina began to feel dazed and slumped to the floor. "Help me," he said to Narezza. "We'll clean her up a bit before we take her to the King's chambers." He eyed the blood spatter on her silk gown. "Too bad this is ruined. But don't worry, she won't need it anymore."

***

The knowledge of real events evaporates like morning mists while tales told by those they most benefit soon serve as the truth. Crina listened as Marku continued.

"After the insurrection of the Boyars, peace prevailed in Ruthenia. In 1389, Brută fell in love with Princess Almira of Galicia. All were happy as preparations for a grand wedding were made."

***

"Shut the door and come in here," said Brută. "It is time."

"Time for what, Sire?" asked Necula.

"You know very well, Vrăjitor. Don't play dumb with me. It has been two years since the problem with the Boyars was resolved. The rest of my subjects have fallen into line. I have arranged to wed Princess Almira of Galicia to align our two kingdoms. She will arrive soon and Crina, though she has proven a pleasant diversion, is no longer needed. I fear the Queen Consort would fail to appreciate the presence of a curtezană in our bed. It is time for this peasant girl to serve her true purpose and take her place in the Grand Hall."

"I understand, Sire."

***

Narezza brought Crina to Necula's chamber. He stood behind a boiling cauldron. "Stay here and do not speak," she said, retrieving a black vial from a niche in the wall behind Necula. Returning to the cauldron, she poured its contents in, along with some ground herbs from the pouch which hung around her neck. Then she dipped a crystal goblet into the boiling concoction, mixing the steaming contents with a crooked finger. Smelling the concoction, she said, "Good, good. Now drink, my girl. Drink that you may prepare." Crina hesitated. "Don't want to please the King, silly girl?" asked Narezza. "You have pleased him many times up until now. Now you can do so forever." Still Crina hesitated. Narezza pointed at her. "This is only a weak sample of what awaits if you don't cooperate. Remember, you could always take Maricara's place. Searing pain swept over Crina. Trembling, she brought the cup to her lips and sipped. The world around her began to swirl before she fell into a deep sleep.

Crina became aware of the faint sound of feet scuffling across the floor. She tried to turn her head toward the direction of

121

the noise, but could not. Maricara's face suddenly appeared over her eyes.

"It is no use, my dearest Crina," Maricara said. "It pains me so to see you lying here." She caressed Crina's cheek. It was as smooth and cold as polished marble. Crina felt nothing. "I have seen this before," said Maricara. "Sadly, Narezza's potion has accomplished its evil purpose." Tears rolled down Maricara's cheek and fell into Crina's eyes. "Now you have tears," said Maricara. The crystal droplets lingered for a moment before vanishing. Maricara leaned very close to Crina and whispered something into her ear as she drifted off.

The next morning, Crina stared across the Grand Hall. Sunlight, cresting over the horizon, shone through the windows leaving a crisp black shadow along each pilaster. Brută strolled across the dais until he stood in front of the pilaster. He looked up at Crina.

"Things are working out as planned. In one month hence, I will wed Princess Almira. Unfortunately," he sighed, "her father will be assassinated and I will become king of Galicia. And let's not forget I have you, my sweet flower. Do you remember today is my birthday? Will you wish me happiness and a long life?"

Transfixed by Crina's beauty, he did not notice the figure clothed in black emerge from the shadows. She thrust a knife deep into his heart with a single blow. He fell to the floor, blood welling from the wound.

Maricara, pulled back her hood and looked up at Crina, perched on the pilaster nearest the dais. "Dearest sister, neither his eyes nor his mind will defile you again. As for the Vrăjitor and his witch who did this to you, I have poisoned them. Their death will be long and painful. Mine will be swift." Dropping the knife, she withdrew a vial from her robes and drank its contents. Clutching her throat, she fell dead

***

That was how it had ended and this began. Incredible sadness overwhelmed Crina. She remembered the words Maricara had whispered to her.

"From this time forward and forever, dear Crina, you will exist as a living statue. You will see and hear, but you will never move again. Soon they will come and take you to the Grand Hall where you will take your place as the most favored among Brută's idols. I am sorry that I was too late to prevent this, but you will be avenged."

Crina turned her attention back to Marku. "I am sure," he said, "you have noticed the brass railing that cordons off this small portion of the sun calendar." Marku rested his hand on the circular fence to his side. "No one is allowed to step on the sunburst at its center, for it marks the King's birthday. You are very lucky, for it is noon and you can see the sun shines directly on it. It seems Brută died of mysterious causes on his birthday in 1389 just a few months before his wedding. Some say he died from an unknown illness or heart attack. Some say he died of complications from his many wounds in battle. We will never know. But we do know he was greatly mourned. Some even say his favorite statui femei, Crina, the Lily, shed a tear in mourning that day. There are those who believe each year on Brută's birthday, the statue cries. Is it true? Decide for yourselves." Marku turned and pointed toward the statue. "Behold the Miracle of Grondo, Crina, the Weeping Maiden." The visitors gasped as they watched a tear appear in the eye of the statue.

Crina gazed down on the visitors. *No, not for him, Maricara. For you.*

123

DARK HARVEST[15]

Jorge gazed over the valley floor as he climbed the steep slope to the tree line of the forested mountain. The sun was brilliant and even though it was just an hour after sunrise, the heat rose up from the green overgrowth drawing beads of sweat out of his forehead. The valley floor was quiet and he could hear birds singing in the forest ahead. As Jorge moved along, he could hear himself breathe. The tangled undergrowth scraped his leggings. This would be a good day he thought.

Usually such bright hot mornings foretold the discovery of many fruits. Jorge was especially good at locating the fruit. The other finders always approached the task uneasily, constantly in fear of the danger that accompanied the finder in his foraging. But for Jorge, finding was a relief. He was good at his job and it freed him from working with the others back at the encampment.

As he struggled up the steep slope, he remembered when he was been chosen to come to this strange world. The quest leaders had sent for him as they had for many other youths. His parents told him that it was his duty to go. The youths in many of the villages were resistant to the quest. Jorge too questioned the worth of this quest but fearing the disapproval of his parents and the quest leaders, he dutifully followed their orders. He could not shame them by fleeing to the wilds. Jorge had always tried to follow the rules set forth by his parents and the village shamans. They were elaborate, covering all aspects of life including one's thoughts. All youths were schooled in them from a very early age. Failure to follow the rules and do one's duty was displeasing and would result in ridicule, punishment or even banishment. The

<hr>

[15] "Dark Harvest" appeared online in *Down In The Dirt*, 12/2021.

thought rules were most difficult and confusing. Even thinking wrong things was bad. God, the omnipotent one, for whom his parents and village shamans spoke, knew all and would condemn those not having the correct thoughts to an eternity of pain and loneliness. As with all youths, Jorge gave in to temptations. He did not often get caught, yet he lived in fear of being found out and knew in his heart that he was bad. Anything new was frightening. New people and new situations always meant new rules and new opportunities for failure.

The quest journey to the far world had been filled with many frightening events. There were many temptations presented to Jorge along the way. Although he had tried to follow all the rules he had learned, he was ever drawn to break them for his own pleasure and amusement. Jorge knew, in order to avoid ridicule and punishment, he must follow every rule set out for him. But, he always failed. He learned to hide and lie about his sins effectively. Although he was successful at fooling those around him, Jorge knew that he was inherently bad and that he had let everyone down, especially God. He could keep many of his sins hidden from people, but not from God, who was all knowing. Jorge had long since given up hope of pleasing God and had accepted that his spirit would be banished to the wastelands after his death.

He envied and despised those who tested the rules, believing that they received too little retribution for their acts. He knew that if he had committed those acts and had been found out, he would have been severely punished. On the trip to the new world, he deviated many times from the rules and lived in dread that he would be found out. He drank to numb his fears. To make up for his failures, he performed his tasks as perfectly as was possible knowing that he was valued only by the measure of his performance.

After a few minutes of climbing, Jorge came upon a small, open area. Such areas were particularly good for finding fruit. Just outside the shadows of the leaves, he found them. There were six, all fine specimens. The fruit was typically black or pink and sometimes brown. This group had two black and four pink. They lay on the forest floor covered by their dark green husks with some of the soft flesh exposed. Red, sticky sap drooled out of various pores in the fruit. These, he realized were very fresh.

As a finder, Jorge found a task suited to his likes. He could work alone and was free to explore his own thoughts as he searched. After a find, he would mark the spot and tally the numbers. Later, the gatherers would come for the harvest. Most finders were uneasy about the job. They were unaccustomed to the fruit and disliked the thought of wandering around the forests alone. Some believed the fruit brought bad luck and that evil things would befall them if they touched it.

After the fruit was tallied and gathered, it was usually sent back to the villages. There, it received much attention. Some villagers, like his parents, rallied around the fruit and pointed to it with pride, citing the greater cause of the quest. Others wept for the destruction of a far world and the loss of a generation of young men to the quest.

Most of this was lost on Jorge. He was content to go about his finding duties feeling neither pleasure nor dismay over the job that so many others hated. After so many years of living with his pain and fears, he learned to drive them deep inside where they rarely surfaced anymore. When they did, he always had drink to numb them. He had a task to complete. He felt nothing save the satisfaction of turning in his locations and tallies knowing that for another day he had gotten by without any trouble.

After finding two more groups of fruit, Jorge returned to camp. He went to the long house to sit on the fringe of the gathers and hunters, drink kava and listen to their tales of heroism. He rarely joined in, knowing they disliked him and resented his presence. This night as had happened on other occasions, he was jeered by a hunter who had too much to drink. Jorge left the long house and returned to his bed in shame. As he lay in his bed, his anger and resentments turned slowly inward. Just before he drifted into unconsciousness, he realize how utterly desolate he was, how he had no worth and how thin and weak was the facade he portrayed to the world. The hopelessness of his life weighed heavily upon him like a rock on his chest. Then, he dreamed his dream: One day while out finding, he would be transformed. Where he was once the finder, he would now be the found. He would lay in the dirt among the leaves and branches until another finder came to tally him and mark his location for the gathers. They would send him home to the village where all those who had criticized him and called him down would march through the streets and sing heroic songs and set him in a place of honor. This transformation that the others feared would be his moment of victory. Only then would his parents, the shamans, and his comrades accept him. Perhaps even God would take pity on him. This is what he longed for, to be freed from the misery of his existence and to gain acceptance. It was his dream of hope, his dream of despair.

The next day, Jorge set out to search for more fruit. The day was cold, dark, and overcast, the kind that he disliked as the light was poor in the forest making finding more difficult. He was just about to enter the forest when he sensed a stillness in the forest he had not experienced before. He moved cautiously into the trees.

He felt the searing pain in his chest before he heard the report of the rifle. The forest floor rose up slowly to meet him. As he lay choking on his blood, he saw a figure with a rifle step out from behind a tree, then the flash of the muzzle. The transformation was complete, he lay dead on the forest floor.

***

The 14 year old Afghan sniper was pleased as he watched the American soldier convulse one last time as the second bullet tore through his torso. He had seen many such men fall at his hands. This one had been near enough to see clearly. Sometimes these men had looks of surprise and horror in their faces, other times they had hatred in their eyes. This was the first time he had seen one smile.

THE USUAL CONCLUSION[16]

"What's the effective oxygen percentage?" Citlali asked. She and Lulana had already consumed two hours of their space suit oxygen supply. They had left their ship on the high plateau and climbed down a narrow ravine. Now, they continued on foot down the sloping plane. Their bulky suits, combined with the planet's rough terrain, slowed their progress.

"Less than five percent," Lulana answered.

"When can we take off our helmets?"

"Perhaps when the level gets to seven percent."

"How long will that take?" asked Citlali.

"At this rate, could take hours unless we find a route with a steeper decline."

"Are you sure we couldn't take them off sooner?"

"Yes," said Lulana. "The laws of physics still apply here. We must reach a point low enough so when you take a breath, the atmospheric pressure is sufficient to fill your lungs. Until then, we will have to wear our helmets or suffocate."

* * *

Citlali surveyed the rubble-strewn landscape. She looked over her shoulder. The plateau loomed far behind. "This would have been a good place for samples," she said, grabbing a handful of pebbles and grit. She examined them in the grainy twilight of the alien planet. "Since we're still on the clock, might as well," she said, opening her sample pouch.

Lulana placed her hand on Citlali's arm. "Why don't we sit for a while? I could use a bit of rest and so could you."

[16] "The Usual Conclusion" appeared in *Our Universes* - a Boyle County Public Library Chapbook published through Sheppard Press, 2019.

"Sure," replied Citlali. She dropped the rocks into the pouch, then sat down, leaning back on a large rock.

"Besides, who's to know?"

"You're right. Who's to know? What was I thinking?" Citlali tossed the pouch aside. She stared into the lambent night sky. "How long do you think the night lasts here?"

Lulana looked up. "I don't know, but we have been out here almost four hours and the stars have barely moved."

"Looks like we're in for a long night."

"I agree. Let's get moving."

* * *

The loose rubble scrunched under Citlali's boots. The plateau was far in the distance. Her knees ached from bracing her legs against the slope as they descended. She paused for a moment before asking, "Can we rest for a moment?"

"Sure," said Lulana. She let her pack slip to the ground, then sat on it. "My backside can't take anymore rocks."

Citlali did the same. After getting comfortable, she asked, "Do you think anyone back home is looking at us?"

"What do you mean?"

"I mean do you think anyone on Earth is looking at the stars this very moment. Looking at this point in the sky?"

"Humans have always looked to the heavens in an attempt to make sense of their place in the Universe," replied Lulana. "Even in the age of interstellar travel with people hard wired into the Web, I'm sure at least one person on Earth is looking at the constellation Pegasus. And they will see where we are, The Great Pegasus Cluster at the tip of his nose. We're in there somewhere, but I don't know the exact location. Won't make a difference to anyone on Earth because this grand swarm of stars appears to them as a mere speck of light."

"Are you sure that's where we are?"

"I think so. I confirmed our location before we dropped out of hyper flight into that pea soup of asteroid rubble.

"I can't believe it," Citlali whispered.

"Yeah, what were the odds of that happening? One in a billion?"

"No. Not that. I meant the sky on this planet, filled with so many stars. When you compare the night sky back on earth to this, sadly, ours becomes thoroughly inadequate. This must be how the Milky Way looks from the inside."

"That's because we are inside the Milky Way."

"Oh, I knew that. Where's my head gone to?

"That's OK. There's a lot to take in."

"When I was very young," said Citlali, "the school from the Rez took us to Tonopah, Nevada. That's the place I first experienced the full wonder of the night sky. More than 7,000 stars were visible. And the Milky Way stretched from horizon to horizon. That's when I decided to become an astronaut."

"Same here," said Lulana. "We went to the Waterberg Plateau in Limpopo. There, I first saw the Southern Milky Way in a sky free from light pollution. I'd never seen so many stars. But it was nothing compared to this. There's gotta be over 100,000 stars visible in this sky."

"At least. Where do you think our solar system is?" Citlali asked.

"Hard to pinpoint exactly without the ship's computers. But it's out there somewhere, though no more than a mere prick of light, with its frail rocks and bubbles of gas circling round it."

"What kind of star mythology do you think a civilization on this planet would've developed?"

"I believe it would've been more extensive," answered Lulana, "but, no more rich and diverse than that of our ancestors."

"How so?"

"On Earth, our ancestors identified shapes in the sky. These became the constellations. Different cultures and countries adopted their own versions. They used them to relate stories of their beliefs, experiences, creation, and mythology. For instance, we have an African folk tale that says a strong-willed girl created the Milky Way. I think it would've been much the same for inhabitants of this world."

"Any chance this strong willed girl was named Lulana?" asked Citlali.

Ignoring the question, Lulana continued. "Her mother refused to give her a portion of the delicious roots she was roasting. The girl became so angry, she snatched the roots from the burning ashes and threw them into the sky. There, the roots glowed as red and white stars, and the ashes became the Milky Way. The path made by a young girl many, many years ago, who threw the bright sparks of her fire high up into the sky, became a road in the darkness. The road remains to this day."

"Oh, she definitely must have been named Lulana," smirked Citlali.

"Anyway, inhabitants of this planet would have created their own myths associated with the sky," said Lulana.

"Would they have believed in God?"

"It stands to reason. Belief in God is widespread and many, many cultures associate God with the sky. Why should the inhabitants of this planet have differed in that respect?"

"That makes sense. I believe in the Great Spirit which is the native American concept of a supreme being or God for want of a better term. Do you believe in God?"

"Sometimes, despite being raised a Christian."

"That is a strange answer."

"My family was killed by the Mwanga Wa Kweli while I was at university. It's been hard to believe in God since then." Lulana stood up. "Come on, we better go."

* * *

They continued walking in the endless twilight until Citlali, overwhelmed with fatigue, slumped to the ground. She checked the view screen on her arm. "We've been out here almost seven hours," she rasped. "My O2 is about spent."

Lulana checked hers. "Mine too." She knelt down next to Citlali.

"We're not going to make it, are we."

"No. We don't have much time left," said Lulana, "perhaps only minutes."

"Do you think the distress call went through before we crashed?"

"Hard to tell, but I think not. That space rubble battered us pretty good before we crashed. Bet you didn't think this would happen to you first time out. Tough luck. Anyway, I don't think it matters much anyway if the distress call went out or not."

"Why is that?" asked Citlali. "If the call went out and they sent a rescue ship, it might still get here in time."

"Sure, *if* the call went out. *If* they sent another ship immediately. I hate to break the news, but that's not the way it's going to play out. You see, we're expendable. Always were. That old scow they sent us out in is evidence enough. Once Wooton Outlands Exploration realizes we crashed, they aren't likely to send a rescue ship."

"I can't believe that."

135

"Look, before they do anything, they will have the accountant run an analysis of the cost of a rescue mission versus writing off the equipment loss and paying out our contract to our next of kin. Guess what? You can bet the numbers won't be in our favor. We won't account for anything more than a footnote in the report. It's happened before."

"Doesn't make sense. This planet seems like a good bet. From what little I have seen, there are ample exportable minerals. Couple that with the potential of a breathable atmosphere and you'd think the Company would jump at the opportunity. Why would they give up so easily?"

"Oh, they won't give up on the planet. Just us. They'll let things cool down a month or two, then find two more volunteers to explore this rock."

"I see." Citlali lay still, sucking in a few labored breaths and fighting back her tears. Finally, she said. "You were talking about the African myth of the Milky Way. The American Indians have their legend also. When the footsteps of their ancestors brought them to that chasm beyond which men venture only once, they vanished from the Earth. But, their spirits journeyed on, creating the pathway of the souls arching across the sky. Each bright star is a campfire blazing where they have paused in their journey. From there, they look down on the people, as they huddle for warmth around the campfire."

"Campfires and roasted roots," said Lulana. "At least they will be well fed."

"I wish we could have built a campfire so those on Earth would know we are looking down on them as we journey on." With a trembling hand, Citlali released the disconnect on her helmet.

"Don't," cried Lulana, reaching for her hand. "there's not enough oxygen, you would only last a few moments."

"But it would be long enough."

"Long enough for what?"

"To see the heavens as I did when I was a child. Not through a plastic visor, fogged by my dying breath, but a final, unfettered look at the sky." Citlali pulled off her helmet and gasped. The sky dazzled above her like the inside of a Fabergé egg profusely encrusted with radiant sapphires, rubies, and diamonds. Only diaphanous veins of black hinted at the cosmic void beyond.

"What do you see?" Lulana asked.

"The essence of God."

Looking up, Lulana reached for the disconnect on her helmet.

Epilogue 1

Satisfied the creatures were either dead or unconscious, Grundu emerged from his hiding place in the rocks. He had seen something fall from the sky and had scrambled up from the deep valley to investigate. Startled to see two creatures in the distance stumbling toward him, he had hidden from sight. From there, he watched as they drew nearer to his hiding place until one fell, quickly followed by the other.

He approached the creatures with caution, his bulbous eyes searching for the slightest movement. Tiny yellow air sacs squeezed out from the breathing slits in his dry, leathery skin. They labored to process the sparse oxygen in the high altitude. Reaching his destination, Grundu hunched over the two creatures sprawled on the ground, examining them carefully for any signs of life. Sensing none, he licked the face of the darker creature, tasting the sweet flesh. Standing up, he raised his head to the sky and stridulated a chant of thanks to the Infinite Being for the gift of fresh meat.

Epilogue 2

"Waddya want, Zlyk?" Ang Fegult growled, as the spindly assistant to the Operations Manager slid through the cubical opening. "Can't you see I'm busy?"

"The Boss has got a little job for you."

"Couldn't he just send me a request?"

"No!" Zlyk barked, "He said he didn't want anything on record until he heard what the Chief Accountant has to say."

"So, spit it out."

"You know that mining exploration ship we just sent out?" asked Zlyk.

"You mean that old beater we sent to the Great Pegasus Cluster?" muttered Ang.

"Yeah. They've gone silent. Only thing we got was a portion of a distress signal when they dropped out of hyper flight. They're either on their way to the other side of the Universe or they have crashed. Either way, the Boss wants you to run the numbers on a rescue mission versus a write off."

"How soon does he need it?"

"He wants your report to send to Okoro in twenty minutes," answered Zlyk.

"So, what's he looking for?"

Zlyk sneered. "The usual conclusion."

DARK MEAT[17]

"Tastes like chicken."

"Give it a break. I don' t see this as a time for humor."

"Ease up on him, Ed, I think he' s just commenting on the food." "Same goes for you too, Jeffrey! Let' s just drop it."

"Hey, I mean it," Albert said as he studied the morsel perched on the tip of his fork. "Though I wouldn't say it tastes like the best chicken I ever had. No, not even close. But chicken just the same. You know, the best I ever had was the fried chicken at Willie Mac's. Man, that was some kind of chicken. Me, I liked the dark meat. You know what they say, 'The closer to the bone, the sweeter the meat'."

"Listen, stupid, nothin' that ever came out of that computerized garbage disposal of a food prep unit ever tasted like chicken or anything else you'd want to eat," Ed grumbled as he stared down at his plate. "No matter how much artificial flavoring it adds and lumpy sauce it dumps on top, and whether it calls it Peking Duck or chicken à la king, it still tastes like hinge grease on rubber bands."

The three sat silently for a few minutes staring down at the meager portions on the plates before them. The harsh glare of the ship's lights made their skin appear wan against the stainless steel of the tabletop.

Then Jeffrey looked up and said, as if the conversation had never paused, "Alligator."

"What?"

[17] "Dark Meat" appeared in *Brief Grislys* published by Apocryphile Press, 2013.

"Alligator. Had it once in Louisiana. That's what this tastes like: alligator." "Damn, not you too!"

"Don't think I ever tasted alligator," Albert declared. "What's it taste like?"

"Little bit like this," Jeffrey cooed, patiently pointing to his plate, "only much, much better. Had it down in New Orleans one Mardi Gras. Alligator étouffée at Boochie's on the Levee.""What's an ate too fay?" Albert asked.

"About the best thing you ever put in your mouth. Comes from the French word meaning 'smothered.' The locals say it tastes like dark-eyed women and zydeco."

"I'm warning you, put a cork in it." Ed growled.

The three again sat in awkward silence, avoiding eye contact. The only sound was the drone of the engines which occasionally sent a shudder rolling through the ship.

"Both of you are wrong," Ed stated emphatically.

Albert and Jeffrey looked up at him inquisitively. He was still glaring at the plate that sat on the table in front of him. Then he looked up and gave each a smug glance."It was in Peru."

Albert and Jeffrey exchanged glances as if to ask each other if Ed had finally gone completely mad.

"In Cuzco. That's where I had it. Guinea pig, first cousin to a rat. That's what this stuff tastes like," he said stabbing a finger at his plate. "The most Godawful stuff you ever put in your mouth. A stringy, foul mess. It's the damn national food down there; like hamburgers back home. It was like eating chunks of bulkhead gasket. I don't even think they skinned the damn things. Tasted like something ugly and dead and it lingered deep in the back of my throat so even half a dozen Pisco Sours couldn't wash out the taste. Just like this stuff." With that he shoved his plate away and put his head down. "Damn that Jürgen," Ed spewed. "Why did that little bastard have to go and screw everything up?"

"Hey, it wasn't all Jürgen's fault," Jeffrey offered timidly. "He had nothing to do with the dark energy drive failure."

"Listen, stupid number two: if Jürgen hadn't been selling spare parts, among other things, on the black market to pay off his gambling debts, we— the crew of Space Freighter 571— wouldn't be in our little predicament now, would we?"

"He's got a point there," Albert chimed in between chews.

"Exactly, if Jürgen hadn't been up to his little tricks, we might have had some real food and something to fix the damn drives," Ed hissed, slamming his fist to the table, rattling the silverware. "If the little jerk hadn't frozen to death while hiding in the deep freeze, I swear I would have strangled him with my own bare hands."

"Well, at least he saved you the trouble," Jeffrey sniped back, "or were you looking forward to it?"

"No, it wasn't like that. But you'll have to admit that he left us in the lurch."

"And . . and it's not like he's not helping in his own way, him . . . being gone and all. You know, one . . . less mouth to feed . . . and . . .and . . ." Albert stammered.

"And what?" Ed spumed, throwing his cup across the room.

They fell into a sullen silence. After a while, Albert— mustering his courage— asked, "How long until we make port?"

"I ran the numbers again," Jeffrey said without looking up. "Nothing has changed. Without the dark energy drives, it will take us about 6 weeks."

"How much is left, Ed?" "How much what?"

"Come on, you know, how much food?"

"Food? Well that's been gone for a week. But if you are referring to Jürgen à la king," Ed snorted, pointing to his plate, "there's about two weeks' worth, if you don't make a pig of yourself.'

"Did you put all of him in the food prep unit?"

"Yes," Jeffrey said quietly as he swallowed the last forkful from his plate. With one sweep of his hand, Ed stuffed the rest of his portion into his mouth and started chewing noisily while glaring wide-eyed at his two companions.

"But what do we do when we run out of Jürgen?" Albert asked plaintively.

Ed looked at Albert and Jeffrey with a wry smile on his face, while spittle, dotted with flecks of dark meat, ran down his chin. "Well, that's certainly food for thought. Ain't it, boys?"

AUTUMN LEAVES[18]

Autumn's wireless headset blared 'You Made Me This Way', causing her throbbing headache to treble in magnitude. *Shouldn't have had a good-luck-with-the-interview party all by myself.*

She tapped the button. "Hi, Mom."

"Is that you, dear?"

"Yes, Mom, who else do you think would be answering my phone? Make it quick, I'm on the road."

"Don't tell me you're still going to that interview."

"Okay, I won't."

"But it's so far away and you've got such a nice job already."

"Mom, I'm tired of being the weekend weather girl and doing remotes on Pilates classes at 6:00 am. I'm 28 and this may be my last chance to get an evening anchor job."

"It's so far away."

"Burlington's only a three and a half hour drive. Right up I-89. It's not that far." *But, far enough.* "I bet you'd love Lake Champlain. Might even see Champy when you come up." *Why did I say that?*

"Who's Champy?"

"Don't have time to explain, Mom. Did I mention I'm on the road? Distracted driving and all that."

"What about David? Are you going to leave him behind? I thought you two might. . . "

"Mom, we'll just have to see."

"Well, I hate to see you pass up such a good prospect."

---

[18] "Autumn Leaves" appeared online in *Teleport Magazine*, 3/21/2020.

Such a good prospect he thought I wouldn't mind if he was doing the horizontal bop with my former BFF Sarah. "I'm saying goodbye now, Mom."

"Love you, dearie."

"You, too."

Autumn tapped the button on the wireless, yanked it off her ear and tossed it in the backseat. *Now for a little peace and quiet.* She dug a finger into her jeans pocket and retrieved the Trazodone tab her hairdresser had given her.

"Just in case you need a little calm-down help," she had said.

Autumn washed it down with the last tepid drops of her Caramel Macchiato. Should be smooth sailing from here.

The fall foliage was at its peak. To enjoy the color, she had left the interstate an hour ago, driving her white Toyota rental west through the Green Mountain Forest. Autumn had plotted a route to take her down roads with the least interruption of the forest. The colors were as vibrant as an over-processed chamber of commerce brochure. *Boston is so gray -- my life is so gray.* The trees closed in on the pavement, leaving a narrow band of deep cerulean sky above. A never ending supply of leaves filled the roadway, swirling in the car's wake. The green of Summer had been replaced with every conceivable shade of red, yellow, purple, black, orange, pink, magenta, blue and brown.

Autumn opened the fresh air vent, allowing the scent of leaves to fill the Toyota. She remembered the visits to Gramma and Grampa Silva's farm in Pennsylvania. They would rake leaves into a huge mound, then she would jump in. The sweet odor of the leaves tickled her nostrils as she floated down into the sweet, soft darkness. She would lie still while they walked around the mound.

"Where did Autumn go?" they asked. "Autumn, where are you?" they called.

She would lie still as long as she could before jumping up, throwing armfuls of leaves into the crisp fall air to their feigned cries of relief. Then, they would grab the rakes and start again. Afterward, they would sit on the porch sipping spiced tea and eating apple turnovers.

She remembered when she was eight and Gramma helped her collect every type of leaf they could find. They searched for the best and brightest leaves, rejecting any blemish. Gramma would say the name of each one as they carefully placed them in a pillowcase. By the time they returned home, Grandpa had set up the old ironing board on the porch. Gramma got out her iron and a roll of wax paper. Grandpa tore squares off the roll while Gramma helped her write each leaf's name on a snippet of index card. Using the iron, they sealed each leaf and label between two sheets of wax paper. Grandpa punched holes in each laminated sheet and helped her put them in a binder.

The road narrowed significantly while Autumn drifted between driving and daydreaming. Leaves covered the pavement. She saw a tattered white sign at the side of the road which read:

Welcome to
THE VILLAGE OF BOSK
Home of the world's largest leaf pile.

I don't remember this place on the map. Why didn't I hook up the Garmin? While she searched for a spot to pull over, she felt around the passenger seat for her phone. A quick check of Google Maps would solve the mystery. Beyond the sign, the road curved to the right and opened into the town square. It was ringed with Victorian era buildings, each painted in a different muted earthy color to enhance the bright fall foliage.

People with rakes were everywhere, filling baskets, bedsheet bundles and anything else that could hold leaves. In some places, the leaves were up to their knees. Ahead, on the right, Autumn saw a sign for the Falling Leaves Café. A lady was sweeping leaves from around the tables on the front sidewalk. She was loading them into a bushel basket. Autumn could not see the curb, so she eased the car over until she felt the soft bump of the front tire against the leaf covered concrete. She was fumbling with her phone when she heard a tap on the passenger side window. Autumn opened it.

"You look like a pumpkin pie latte and an apple fritter," the lady said, leaning on her rake.

"No thanks. I think I missed my turn. Just trying to figure out where I am."

"Well you're in the Village of Bosk, home of the world's largest leaf pile. Perhaps you're right where you're supposed to be."

"Is this Vermont 125?"

"Oh no, you're quite a ways from there," the woman said. "Come on, have a sip and a snack and we'll get it all sorted out."

Autumn checked her watch. She had allowed for a leisurely pace and pit stops. The Caramel Macchiato she finished two hours ago was letting her know now was a good time.

"Have you got a public restroom?"

"Inside at the back on the left," said the lady, nodding toward the café door. "I'll have your latte and fritter ready when you get back. I'm Molly."

"Autumn Silva."

"That's a pretty name. And so appropriate for leaf season," said Molly.

"Thanks. Okay to leave my car here?"

"Sure."

The sidewalk under the tables had filled with leaves by the time Autumn returned. Her latte and fritter were waiting. She sat down. Leaning forward, she inhaled its rich aroma before taking a sip. *Wow, this is good.* Molly had started filling another bushel basket. She leaned the rake against the wall and sat down across from Autumn.

"It looks like you've cornered the market on leaves," Autumn said, watching the townsfolk busily raking. "The trees still look like they haven't dropped a leaf."

"Maybe we just got the most prolific and fast leaf makin' trees," said Molly. "What brings you here this day?"

"I'm heading up to Burlington to interview at Channel 3. They've got an evening news anchor spot open."

"We don't have nothin' like that, but we sure got a nice little radio station: WAUT AM. You ever listened to it?"

"Can't say that I have."

A steady line of people walked past carrying leaves, eventually joining lines entering from other streets around the town square. Autumn found the gentle sound of their conversations punctuated with laughter comforting. They were all headed to a ramp which lead up to a platform. It gleamed white against the blue sky. Reaching the top, they dumped their leaves into a chute which sent them cascading onto the largest pile of leaves Autumn had ever seen. The medley of colors, ranging from bright tangerine to deep red, glowed in the sunlight.

Too bad I couldn't get a gig here. "You guys weren't kidding about the largest pile of leaves in the world, were you." said Autumn. "How tall is that thing?"

"Oh, it gets about 30 feet high, I guess."

"Doesn't the wind play havoc with a pile of leaves that high?"

"Never has."

"Then what do you do after you pile up all the leaves?" asked Autumn.

"Then someone jumps in."

"You get someone to jump into a 30 foot high pile of leaves?"

"Yes."

"Now, you're pulling my leg. Have a good laugh at the expense of the city girl."

"No so. It's like jumping into an old fashioned downy feather mattress. Besides, it's a great honor."

"I'll take your word for it." *Really? Like a feather mattress!* Autumn took a bite of her apple fritter. Its sweet flavor with a hint of cinnamon reminded her of Grandma's apple turnovers. While watching the various lines of townsfolk converge and march up the ramp, she traced the outline of the bright red maple leaves embedded in epoxy on the tabletop. After adding leaves to the growing pile, they worked their way back down to join the growing crowd around its base.

When the end of the line reached the Falling Leaves Café, Molly stood up. "Time to take our leaves to the pile," she said, hefting a bushel basket overflowing with leaves. "You coming?" she asked.

"I guess so," said Autumn, scooting her chair back from the table. She drank down the last of her latte, then started to walk toward the pile.

"Aren't you forgetting something?" Molly asked.

"What's that?"

"Leaves! You haven't got any leaves. You can't go to the pile without your leaves. Grab a couple of handfuls and put them in that," she said, pointing to the half-filled bushel basket.

Autumn scooped up some leaves and dropped them in. She picked up the basket and followed Molly. They caught up with the end of the line at the base of the ramp. A steady flow of people with empty containers were descending as Autumn and Molly made their way to the top.

"This is Autumn," Molly repeated to each one coming down. "She just got here."

Autumn acknowledged each cheery 'hi' and 'hello'.

By the time they reached the top, the townsfolk had formed a wide circle around the leaf pile. Molly dumped her leaves into the chute and they disappeared over the lip, a few floating momentarily in the afternoon breeze.

"Now you," Molly directed.

Autumn edged up to the chute and turned her basket upside down, shaking it to make sure every leaf was dispatched. The townsfolk cheered wildly. Autumn waved to more cheers.

She turned toward Molly. "What now?"

"You jump."

"What did you say?"

"You jump. Didn't I tell you the last one to add her leaves to the pile is the one who jumps?"

"No!"

The crowd below began to chant, "Jump, Autumn, jump!"

"Oh, my bad," said Molly. "I thought I did. Nevertheless, you are the last one, you have to jump."

"No, I don't!" Autumn protested.

"Jump, Autumn, jump!"

"Don't worry," reassured Molly. "It's just like jumping into the leaf pile at your grandparents'."

"Jump, Autumn, jump!"

"But I've got my interview. . ." pleaded Autumn.

"I'm sorry, you won't make it. You're right where you're supposed to be."

"Jump, Autumn, jump!"

"No, no," Autumn whispered, backing away from Molly. Her foot landed on the down slope of the chute.

"Jump, Autumn, jump!"

Trying to right herself, Autumn backpedaled furiously. She fell backwards into the crisp fall air. A cheer arose from the townsfolk. She felt only a gentle nudge when she hit the leaf pile -- *Molly was right. Just like falling into a feather mattress* -- then sank down into the sweet, soft darkness.

***

Autumn looked down into the ravine at the end of the pavement. The crushed and burned out carcass of the white Toyota was now fully covered by the leaves. Smiling, she headed toward the town square for a latte and an apple fritter with Molly.

THE GREEN COIL[19]

"Waddya think that's about?" asked Ash. "I hope they ain't planning to eat us."

"Shut up, Ash. If they were gonna eat us, we'd be dead already."

The chant continued for some time until without warning the Indios fell silent. A tall, gaunt figure, with features like the Indios, emerged from the jungle carrying a large communal bowl. He held it out. One by one, the Indios each took a drink. Then they held the bowl out to Ash.

He looked at Lynda. "What should I do?"

"You asked for something to drink, didn't you?" she barked. "Better not risk getting these folks upset. Besides, if you can smoke yuyo, you sure as hell can take a sip of whatever that stuff is."

"I guess you're right," conceded Ash. He took the bowl in his shaking hands and took a sip. Grimacing, he held the bowl out for Lynda, who brought it to her lips. The bitter concoction squirmed down her throat.

The Indios began to sway, murmuring in raspy whispers, "Hwarro… Hwarro… Hwarro…" Lynda sensed a deeper, more sinister underlying drone. It seeped into her soul. The Indios slumped to the ground. They thrashed in the amber glow of the fire, arms melting into their torsos, legs fusing together.

Lynda's head was reeling. The Indios' flesh began to quiver as they thrust their heads back, jaws straining open, cheeks splitting at the corners of their mouths. From each, a sleek glistening snake emerged, leaving behind a flaccid sheath of skin.

[19] "The Green Coil" appeared online in *HauntedMTL*, 10/17/2021.

The snakes writhed in a knotted coil at her feet. Fangs sank deep into her legs. Lynda now grimly realized the tall figure was the Hwarro of the Indios' chanting.

"Lynda," his loathsome voice throbbed in her head. His black eyes focused on her. Hwarro held out his bony hands, beckoning.

"Run Ash!" Lynda screamed, bolting into the jungle. She ran headlong into the black, thrashing through the vegetation. It tore her flesh and snarled her feet. Fangs bit at her. She could hear Ash behind stumbling, gasping for air between shrieks of pain.

"Lynda," Hwarro whispered in her soul.

* * *

Unaware of time and distance, Lynda ran until she thought her lungs would burst. Finally, she reached the river, lurching free from the constriction of the jungle vegetation. Having grown accustomed to the perpetual dusk inside the green labyrinth, the sun blinded her eyes. Legs and arms, whether from fatigue or venom, refuse to obey and she fell headlong to the rocks and sand at the water's edge.

Lynda thought she could hear Ash whimpering. "Ash, are you there?" Lynda attempted to call out. Her voice was a feeble whisper. Lying on the riverbank, unable to move, she stared at the sand, realizing it wasn't really sandy colored. She could see all the grains in their infinite spectrum of colors nestled around the stones and the rotting bits of wood. Across the river, where it bowed away from the sand bar, the rainforest rose up to meet the sky. The river had cut an angry swath in the red soil at its base, exposing boulders and roots.

"Lynda," Hwarro laughed.

She couldn't hear Ash's whimpers anymore. "Ash," she rasped again.

Before passing out, she heard Hwarro's evil, beckoning whisper, "Lynda."

She awoke to excruciating pain. Ants swarmed over her, biting, and tearing at her flesh. She knew they would carry the pieces back to their colony to feed their larvae. She wondered how long it would it take to strip the meat clean from her bones. "Ash," she rasped. No answer. Lynda was relieved. She knew the ants were devouring him also and she didn't want to see it. She wondered if Hwarro whispered to the ants, calling their names?

Lynda could no longer feel her arms or legs. It made no difference. She slithered forward, shedding what remained of her bleeding husk of skin. Her scales glistened in the sun.

Joining Ash, they glided into the dense vegetation of the jungle.

There, in the shadows, Hwarro hummed to her his soft lullaby of welcome.

JUST BUSINESS[20]

"I said, I'm coming up on the perimeter," Vel rasped into his com. He pressed it tightly to his ear.

"Go to .he .ollag .ate , I... bribe. .he ..ard to .et you in," crackled the speaker.

"Basset, did you say the Mollag Gate?" Vel shouted over the wind. "Say again, can't hear a damn thing with all this noise." Static filled his ear.

Vel turned his collar up against the chill, surging wind that whipped through the crooked, crumbling streets leading to Nova Barataria. The smuggler he bribed to bring him there had landed his space junk in the deserted old Port of Barataria. The gusts raked across the uneven pavement and rough walls of the old town, sounding like the cough of a dying man. In the relative silence between bursts, he listened for the other sound that had plagued his journey across the galaxy. It had become increasingly faint since leaving Regla 7. Now that he could not hear it or feel its icy fingers tearing at his soul, he held some hope he was free of the withering assault.

As he worked his way through the crumbling buildings, he tugged at the strap of the heavy backpack, trying to find some relief from the dull pain that soaked into his shoulders. He hoped he had understood Basset's message.

Ahead, the thin glow of streetlights reflected off the transparent dome. There, he hoped to find some relief in the light and bustle of the city. The walled perimeter loomed ahead. He followed the pavement until it disappeared under the vast Mollag

[20] "Just Business" appeared online in *Soft Cartel*, 8/10/2018.

entrance gate. To his left was a security station and a pedestrian turnstile entrance.

Vel presented the false identification he had purchased on Regla 7. After a cursory review, the guard sneered and moved a lever, rotating the rusty turnstile halfway open, the pivot emitting a hoarse squeal. Resigned, Vel squeezed into the narrow opening, the thick tines of the turnstile poking his ribs. Once inside, the guard moved the lever ever so slightly so the squeal turned into a long, shuddering groan. Once again it stopped, leaving a narrow gap for Vel to exit.

"At least put some lube on that damned thing," he muttered, squeezing out into a dark alley. The lights of the city bled in at the far end. The groan of the turnstile was still ringing in his head as he stepped into the market square.

Nova Barataria had been a popular port of call for freebooters for over a millennium. It served as a safe haven for those who indiscriminately plundered the weaker planetary systems too insignificant for, or resistant to, the protection of the galactic trade alliance.

Every marketplace in the galaxy had its own distinct personality. Vel found Nova Barataria's particularly offensive. As he entered, a Dushraki butcher sliced the neck of a yowling gurang hanging by its hind tentacles from the roof of an open air stall. The animal soon fell silent as its thick blood drained into a filthy carafe. An angry knot of anxious customers swelled in the congested pathway, drawn by the pungent aroma. They clamored, like a ravenous animal, for a drink of the intoxicating fluid. Their cries reminded Vel of Tholian jackals attacking their prey. Suddenly, he felt a tug at his backpack. Fearing a brazen thief was trying to steal its contents even while it was on his back, Vel pulled his dirk and whirled around to see the laughing face of a gaunt Clodian.

Vel studied the wrinkled face. "Axolo?" he asked.

"Vel Janders, I wouldn't drink none of that juice," he bellowed in a high pitched voice over the din of the crowd. "Your brains won't work right for a cycle, not to mention your innards. Come on friend, let's find a quiet spot and get a proper drink."

"I'm not your friend. I'm looking for Jehr Basset."

"He's usually over at the Blue Slug. I can take you there." Axolo leaned in close. "Best not leave that exposed friend," he hissed through bright fuchsia gills, motioning to Vel's backpack. "I could hold it for you." His voice was barely audible in the noise of the crowd.

Vel shrugged his backpack off, holding it tight against his chest. "I told you, I'm not your friend. I'll hang on to it, if you don't mind."

"Just trying to help," soothed Axolo. Turning, he pushed into the throng.

Vel fell in behind his gaunt companion. They walked along makeshift streets lined by cobbled stalls where merchants hawked their wares to the desperate and displaced. Strange hands pushed back as he squeezed through the rabble. The odor of vomit and spice filled his nostrils. The cacophony of the market habitués was deafening, pounding inside Vel's head until he thought his skull would burst.

Finally, they arrived at the grimy drinker at the far side of the square. Axolo stepped aside and motioned for Vel to go inside. Just then the door flew open, hinges squawking in protest, nearly knocking them to the ground. A squat Kroyn stumbled out. Axolo quickly grabbed the door with a bony hand and motioned Vel inside. The dimly lit room was packed with denizens in varying states of stupor. Many languished on the cushions that ringed the walls, while others teetered at the bar or slumped at tables. Music blared, almost drowning out the din of arguments and laughter. The cacophony jangled inside Vel's head, torturing his already raw nerves.

"Back there," Axolo said, pointing to an alcove at the far end.

Vel walked carefully through the jumble of tables, not wanting to provoke any of the revelers. Reaching the opening, he hesitated, wondering if Basset was there or Axolo had some mischief in mind. Vel lowered a hand to his dirk.

"Go on Janders. If I had wanted to do something, you'd be dead by now. Basset hasn't got all night," sneered Axolo, nudging Vel forward.

A door within slid open. Axolo shoved Vel in the back, causing him to stumble forward into the room. The door slapped shut behind. At an ornate desk in the corner of the sumptuously appointed room, sat Jehr Basset. An attractive young female, dressed only in jewelry, reclined next to him, holding the end of his golden chibouk. He took a puff.

"Come in, Vel," said the pale lump of a man, exhaling a plume of blue smoke, "or should I call you by that name on the fake identification in your pocket? What is it? Gom Flant? Must be. That's the name I gave to the guard. Not very friendly, is he?"

"No."

"And you can take your hand off that knife," said Basset. "We fellow Earthers must look out for one another, wouldn't you agree?" He motioned to the woman who took the chibouk and disappeared through a door behind Basset.

"Yes," conceded Vel.

"Yes," repeated Basset, "indeed." For a moment, he studied the rangy freebooter, who displayed a barely perceptible, yet definite, haggard look around the eyes. "The name Vel Janders," Basset continued, "used to belong to one of the best freebooters in the galaxy. Looks like things have changed. Fallen on hard times? Come sit down and tell me what's going on. How about a glass of water? It's real, from a glacier in the mountains high above the city, not like that reclaimed stuff they strain through an old sock and sell out on the street." He filled a cup from a crystal pitcher and slid it across the table.

"Don't put yourself out," said Vel, releasing his grip on the dirk. He settled into a chair across the table, dropping his backpack to the floor. Reaching forward, he grabbed the cup and gulped the water down.

Basset leaned back in his chair. "How long has it been, Vel? Six or seven earth cycles? Let me see." He paused as if in thought before continuing. "Oh yes, you were hightailing it out of Daglos 4, leaving me to face the Grand High Commissioner. I thought you and I had an agreement."

"I felt the need to renegotiate. Just business, Jehr. You understand. From the look of things, you did okay. You've put on a few pounds, got some shiny things to keep you company. From the look of things, I'd wager you aren't eating at any of those stalls in the Market."

"You would be correct in that assumption. And yes, I suppose it was just business. But enough of reminiscing, I'm interested in current events. Arriving under the cover of darkness in a grimy space junk. What happened to the Kuró Maru? I loved that ship."

"Sold it and my name to the new Vel Janders on Regla 7. Got just enough to pay for new identification credentials and for passage here."

"Too bad. Had you brought it here," said Basset, "I would have surely paid you more." He paused, eying Vel. "So what can I do for you? I know. Perhaps you are in the hunt for a lustomaton, the young lady who was just here is one of my new models. They're cleaned and serviced regularly."

"I didn't come here for a galbot," barked Vel.

"What then?"

"Basset, I need to get out of here."

"So soon?" asked Basset, feigning surprise. "And we only just started to rekindle old friendships. Axolo will be disappointed."

"I'm serious, Jehr."

"I heard rumors of an incident on Hax. You weren't mixed up in that, were you? One shouldn't get at cross purposes with Haxans. As I understand it, they lean toward the occult. I hear they can be quite tenacious and nasty, resorting to maleficia, when it comes to retribution for transgressions."

"I don't have time for chit chat."

"I do," said Basset, leaning forward. His tone had turned serious. "I heard an important religious artifact was stolen. Know anything about that?"

"I was there to barter for some Galowi. As you well know, there are certain collectors across the galaxy who will pay handsomely for rare animals and Galowi are popular among them. While drinking joukjouk with my suppliers…"

"I believe the proper term is poachers," Basset interrupted.

"…they began talking about the Śarīra."

"The Śarīra. I thought that was a myth," said Basset. "Isn't it purported to be a crystalline sphere found among the cremated ashes of Tala, the first god-empress of Hax, endowed with…"

"Yeah, yeah, yeah and so on. At first, I thought it was the joukjouk talking, but they swore it was real. So like any good freebooter, I dared them to show it to me."

"And?"

"I followed them through the jungle outside the city, wondering if they intended to kill me and divvy up the spoils. We arrived at a sheer rock face that towered at least 500 meters above the forest. A narrow set of carved stairs switchbacked upward into the dark. They refused to go any further so I continued alone."

"Aren't you the brave one," taunted Basset.

"About halfway up, the stairs flattened into a small ledge, leading to an entrance chiseled into the rock face. It wasn't much more than a hole surrounded by a few crude carvings. I went in, feeling my way along the twisted passage until it opened into a large chamber. It was filled an undulating light emanating from an altar at the back.

"At once, I knew the Śarīra was the source. A mesmerizing chant breathed by a thousand unseen voices filled my head. In the flickering glow, the carved statues lining the walls seemed to sway in perfect unison."

"So you snatched up the bauble?" asked Basset. "I thought you had better sense than that. I had you pegged as more of a genteel trader in the grey commodities market than an out-and-out tomb raider."

"All that stuff in the cave had me thinking crazy," Vel said, smiling. "I thought I could get away with it."

"And how did that work out for you?"

"Seemed like a good idea at the time. But here I am sitting here with you. What do you think?"

"You tell me," said Basset.

"Something started dogging me after I left Hax. I couldn't see it, but I could hear it, I could feel it. A horrible voice wailing inside my head, sometimes faint, sometimes thundering. It made me feel like something was crushing my soul."

"I didn't think freebooters had souls," said Basset.

"Well as for you, that could be entirely the case."

"Go on."

"As I was saying, no matter how fast or how far I went, it was always screaming always squeezing."

"Sounds to me, no pun intended, like the Haxans conjured up a haunter to sing your sins."

"Whatever it was, I lost it on Regla 7 when I sold my name and the Kuró Maru. My guess is the haunter-thing followed the scent of the few Galowi I had left in the hold."

"Plausible. And just what is it you want from me?" asked Basset.

"A new identity, passage to a free port and enough credits to get me back on my feet. All free from the scrutiny of the galactic trade alliance, of course."

"You don't want much, do you."

"Should be easy for someone with your resources," said Vel.

"A new identity? Didn't you just buy one?"

"I don't fancy embarking on a new career as Gom Flant. I need something a little more punch. I was thinking of something like Gunder Maks."

"It'll cost you."

"Well, I've used up most of my credits…"

"Then it sounds like you're out of luck. Maybe you can muck out some butcher stalls in the Market until you save up enough," laughed Basset.

"… but, as I was going to say before you interrupted, I might have something…" Vel reached into his backpack and pulled out an object wrapped in cloth.

"Don't pull anything smart," warned Basset.

Vel set the object on the table, letting the cloth fall away. Immediately, the room was flooded in light. Basset drew in a deep breath as he gazed in wonder at the Śarīra.

"…left of value to trade," finished Vel. "You interested?"

"So it's true."

"Of course. Now, how about it?"

"Why not put it on the market yourself?"

"This is all I have left," Vel said, pointing to the Śarīra, "after spending all my credits getting here. As it was, I was running on fumes when I got to Regla 7. It took every credit I received from the sale of my old name and the Kuru Maru to buy a new identity and secure passage here on that space junk. I don't have the resources to market it myself."

"Why did you come here?" asked Basset.

"Thought I'd cut you in for old times' sake."

"More likely, this was the only place you could go where the galactic trade alliance wouldn't arrest you on sight."

"Does it matter?" asked Vel.

"Mighty risky, this Śarīra business. Wouldn't want a haunter-thing, as you call it, singing in my ear."

"I told you, I lost it on Regla 7. Haven't heard the faintest trace of it here. With your connections, you'll find a buyer and be counting your credits in no time. You should realize a tidy profit, if I am guessing right about what you are going to offer me."

Basset leaned back in his chair, staring intently at the Śarīra. "I will make one non-negotiable offer. No conversation, take it or leave it."

"Agreed."

"In exchange for the Śarīra, I will provide passage on my private transport to a free port of my choosing. There, one hundred thousand credits, untraceable and accepted anywhere in the galaxy, as well as your new identity will be waiting. Do you accept?"

Vel sat silent for a few moments. Knowing Basset had him over a barrel, he muttered, "Yes."

* * *

The transport was ready to lift off when Basset's face appeared on the comscreen. "You'll be pleased to know I've already found a taker for the Śarīra."

"You'll be lucky to be rid of it," spat Vel. "Now can we get this tub on its way?"

"…and tell you there has been a slight change of plans. You'll be sharing the ride with another passenger."

"No! We had an agreement," Vel growled.

"Of course we did, but I decided to renegotiate. You should understand that. Just business, you know."

"You bastard," hissed Vel, frantically searching the control console.

"Don't waste your energy," said Basset, "everything's been preprogrammed. You can't change anything. You'll leave as soon as your trip companion arrives."

"When will that be?" huffed Vel. "The sooner I'm rid of Nova Barataria, the better."

"Just about now," answered Bassett, as the airlock door hissed open. "Oh, by the way, the first stop is Hax." A thin, spectral figure, clasping the Śarīra in its withered hands, stepped inside. The airlock slapped shut as the transport lurched upward

"No! You can't do this," screamed Vel, but his words were drowned out by the haunter's shrieking.

FEEDING THE BIRDS

I am sure the sun is up there because it's light enough to see almost everything. It gets pitch black at night though. You can't see nothing. Seems like the clouds have been hanging over everything for such a long time. Sure is dark inside the house even with all the shades up and the curtains pulled back.

Dad's in his easy chair. He looks peaceful. Wonder where Mom is. She's probably in the kitchen or out back on the porch.

It's been quite a while since I've been home. After the Koronides meteor struck, everything went crazy. They said it was damn near as big as the one that killed the dinosaurs. I didn't want to leave Mom and Dad, but after the destruction the chaos started, they took all of us young people to serve in what they called the Homeland Emergency Contingent. That's a fancy term for a forced labor corps. I had just turned fourteen when they took me. I spent three years in HEC trying to rebuild what they call the essential infrastructure. We didn't make much progress as far as I could see.

Got a letter from Mom about a year ago. They haven't gotten the phones working yet. It had taken almost a full year to find to me. She said Dad and her had got the rigids and asked if I could come home. People started coming down with it about six months after the meteor hit. They say that it must have come from some genetic mutation the meteor brought in. If you get it, your body starts to get stiff to the point where you can't move at all. Then you die.

After I got Mom's letter, I packed up that night and snuck out of the barracks. I guess I could be considered a deserter. I was working in Spokane and set out for Kentucky, hitching rides when I could, but mostly walking. Found a mule near the Kansas wastelands and rode it for a while till something that looked like a cross between a bat and a coyote attacked us and killed it. I've been walking ever since.

You would think there would be a lot of deserters, since we were all conscripted. Not true. Times are tough and in the HEC, you get two squares and a safe place to sleep, so not many conscripts leave. I'm not too worried they'll come looking for me, though. They don't have enough people to spare a search party for one homesick hillbilly.

When I was traveling, I tried to make good time during daylight. I didn't want to be out in the dark. Too dangerous. Everyone knows bad things roam about at night. When it was time to sleep, I tried to find some place to shelter, like a house or a barn or a shed. In the wastelands, that was hard to do because almost everything got tore up pretty bad when Koronides hit. Outside of the wastelands, a lot of places got burned down in the food riots. Human scavengers took over what remained. They would sooner kill you and eat you as look at you. Sometimes the only thing I could find was what was left of a tree to sleep in.

There were lots of things that slowed me down on my way home. The biggest thing was bridges, or where bridges used to be. Another big one was coming up on some type of new animal that I had never seen before. Seems like the meteor affected animals too. Then there was just plain struggling through the pain to keep moving.

Bridges that were blocked with broken down vehicles, or worse, fallen down, were big trouble. When a bridge was blocked, it took considerable time and effort to pick my way through the wrecks, leaving me open to attacks. If the bridge had fallen down, I had to climb down one side, get across whatever they built the bridge to cross and climb back up the other side. That wasn't fun doing it with fingers not working their best and stiff knees. At the bottom, if it was water I had to cross, I never knew what was lurking underneath that was gonna try and eat me. The best thing to do was try to make a raft or something to float across.

The trouble with running up on a new type of animal I hadn't seen before was about like trying to swim across a river. I never knew if it's gonna try to eat me or not, so I had to figure that out before anything else. Sometimes I could just shoo it off, sometimes I had to run and hide. Of course running with stiff knees was very hard and painful. Sometimes I had to shoot it but my fingers weren't working too well, which affected my aim. But, I never wanted to shoot it unless there was nothing else to try. That's because I wanted to save my bullets as they are hard to come by. Another reason I didn't want to shoot it is if I didn't kill it with the first shot, it might start to scream, inviting more to come for dinner. Most times, I tried to hide till the coast was clear.

There's Mom sitting out back on the bench. She's holding the large wooden bowl she keeps her birdseed in. It's empty. Looks like the birds have been working on her quite a bit. I'll see if there's a bag of birdseed in the pantry. If there is and I got the energy, I'll drag it out and fill up her bowl so the birds will leave her alone for a while.

I'm awfully tired. Won't be long for me now. After I fill the birdseed bowl, I reckon I'll sit down and keep her company till the birds pick us both clean.

THE SUBJECT

Blackness gave way to dim grey light. The subject heard more snips, then saw more light. The acrid odor of ozone and chemicals filled his nostrils. *Where am I?*

"Relax friend, while I remove the last of your bandages. It will take a moment before your eyes will be able to focus. Try not to look directly into the light."

The subject felt cool air across his face. His eyes struggled with the amber glob of light that hovered above his face. Slowly, it resolved into an oil lamp. Though dim, its light seared his eyes. As he turned his eyes away, an unfamiliar face appeared from the shadows. *Who are you?* The subject tried to speak, but only a ragged wheeze came from his lips.

"Perhaps a sip of water will soothe your throat. Your vocal cords are stiff, but they will soon be right. Wait a moment." The face and lamp disappeared into the swathe of mottled shadow.

The subject stared into the dappled grey void. *Come back.! What happened? I remember. There was the noise of people about. Many people. I could see their faces; cruel faces, laughing faces, somber faces. Suddenly I was falling. A gasp from the crowd, then blackness.*

The face and the oil lamp returned to his view. A hand holding a cup appeared out of the gloom. "Here, take a sip of this. Some water with a dram of brandy to warm you. You had a nasty turn, but you will be all right now. Better than ever, I might venture to say."

The subject lifted his unsteady head until the cup touched his lips. He tasted a hint of bitter fruitiness as the concoction flowed over his tongue. He continued to drink until the cup was drained. A warmth grew in his stomach and spread outward. "Mahhhhh..." he rasped.

"You want some more?"

The subject nodded.

"Good, good indeed. Yes, you shall have some more." The cup withdrew from his lips as the face and hand disappeared once again.

The subject tried to sit up but was held fast. *What is this? I remember, my hands were tied before.*

The face returned, "Pay no mind to the restraints. Just a precaution. Couldn't have you moving around too much after the procedure. But soon enough we'll have you up and about. Now drink some more of this."

Drinking eagerly from the cup, the subject drank, savoring the growing warmth in his stomach. His eyes grew heavy. Before he slipped into the silent blackness, he heard, "Oh, I put a little something extra in your cup to help you sleep."

The subject awoke to the amber glow of the lantern. Forgetting his bonds, he reached out. His joints were stiff. To his surprise, a slender, pale hand glided into his view. It was unfamiliar yet seemed to move at his will. *What is this?* Fingers, long and delicate, quivered in the meager light. The nail beds were tinged in blue. Tentatively, he moved the thumb, then each finger in turn. *I do not recognize these, but they move as if they are mine.* A bright pink welt dotted with scab remnants formed a boundary between the fine pale flesh of the hand and the skin of the wrist and forearm. *What has happened?*

"Aren't they lovely, my friend? Like the fingers of a sculptor."

The subject brought his hands to his face. Unsteady fingers crept over unfamiliar flesh. He could sense the light pressure of the fingertips tracing along, despite the dull numbness of the skin. Fingertips raked over the whiskers on his jaw. *I have touched my face hundreds, no thousands, of times and not felt this countenance. How can this be?* Above his eyes he felt a crusty welt. He let out a gasp. He traced it through the soft stubble along either side of his scalp. *What has happened?*

"The scar will hardly be noticeable once the healing process is finished."

The healing process? Was I injured? Wait, I remember. Yes, falling. And the crowd was jeering. And burning around my neck, I couldn't breathe! He looked at the face in the light. A raspy, unfamiliar whisper welled up in his throat. "Am I dead?"

"No, what do you remember?"

"I... I was hanged. Am I in hell?"

"Not at all. This is my surgery. I brought you here and restored you, so to speak."

"Restored me? I don't understand."

"Of course you don't, few can or ever will."

"Who are you?"

"Call me Victor, friend. Victor Frankenstein."

REWOUND[21]

Dane Hartdegen had not seen his twin brother, Clarke, in at least fifteen years. That had been at the funeral of their mother. Two weeks later, Clarke left his very lucrative research position in Silicon Valley to go 'off the grid' as he explained in a cryptic, one sentence email. Dane drove up to Santa Barbara only to find Clarke had moved out of his apartment, leaving no forwarding address. Calls and texts to his cell phone went unanswered, as did emails. He just disappeared.

Now, Dane found himself driving down a narrow Nebraska road about a hundred miles out of anywhere, checking his GPS for the spot where he should find a dirt path that would lead to his brother. He had received a letter four days earlier from Clarke, saying it was imperative he come right away. It had included nothing else other than the coordinates and instructions to turn left and go to the end of the path. It was postmarked Harrisburg, Nebraska. At first, Dane thought it might be a hoax, but immediately decided no one he knew had enough initiative to construct anything so elaborate. He was angry at the notion his brother would just issue him a summons to appear after fifteen years of silence. That took some nerve. He thought to ignore Clarke's letter, but curiosity and resentment got the better of him, so he reluctantly bought an airline ticket to the Cheyenne Regional Airport. He made up his mind to scorch Clarke if it turned out to be a wild goose chase.

He rented a car and set out. The gently rolling farm fields of Wyoming transitioned seamlessly into the gently rolling farm

---

[21]"Rewound" was presented as a Podcast on *Tall Tale TV,* 1/17/2022.

fields of Nebraska. After an hour and a half, he reached Harrisburg, then headed north until he reached the GPS coordinates. There, he found the dirt path heading out to the left, disappearing over a low rise. He began to feel some relief that this probably was not a wild goose chase, but he still resolved to rip his brother a new one. On the other side, the path stretched ahead through an array of solar panels. His perturbation at the prospect of confronting his brother after all these years increased as he bumped along.

A mile and a half later, the path ended at a small building. It looked like a concrete outhouse with a steel door. He parked next to a white panel van. The dust caught up, swirling around the windshield. He waited until it settled before he got out. The entrance sat at the base of a low, broad hill. He looked around. No one in sight. He peeked in the driver's side window of the van. Nothing. He walked up to the structure. A double door sat recessed one foot into the concrete. Taped to the door was a handwritten note reading, 'Push the button'. An arrow pointed to the right. Shielding his eyes from the bright Nebraska sun, Dane found a small intercom box. He studied it for a moment, gathering courage. He decided to see this thing through no matter what the consequences and pushed the button.

Nothing happened. He pushed the button again, anger welling up. He was about to turn away when a scratchy voice came over the intercom. "Hi Dane, been a long time."

"Clarke?"

"Who else? Look up at the camera so I can see your face." Dane looked up to where the overhang met the wall and saw the glint of a lens in the shadows. "Dane, you haven't aged a day, since I saw you last."

"Clarke, what the hell is this all about? I haven't seen your sorry mug or heard so much as a peep from you in fifteen years." Dane heard a click, then the door swung open. A rush of cold air poured out. It was followed by an old man.

Dane stared at the balding, white haired figure. He looked like Clarke only older, much older. "Who are you?"

"Dane, It's me."

The voice sounded like Clarke's. "Me who?" asked Dane.

"Me, Clarke, your twin brother. Your older brother by three minutes."

"No way in hell my brother Clarke would be an old broke down reprobate like you. Where is he? No more BS. Tell me where Clarke is or I'll have the Nebraska State Patrol out here in a heartbeat."

"I know you are finding this hard to process, but I am your brother. A lot has happened in the last fifteen years. There's things I need to tell you." He reached out for Dane, who recoiled.

Dane wondered what he had gotten himself into. "Not so fast with the touchy, touchy. I don't know you or what you're up to. I came here to find my brother Clarke and if I don't see him right now, I'm gonna call the police." Dane reached into his pocket and pulled out his cell phone.

The old man pulled his arm back and blurted, "Syndactyly!"

"What?"

"Syndactyly, the fusion of two or more digits of the feet. An unusual trait in humans. Something you and I share as twins. The second and third toes on our right foot are webbed, to be exact."

"Clarke could have told you that."

The old man kicked off his shoe and pulled the sock off his right foot. "When we were eighteen, you and I got tattoos on those very same toes. 'Dane' on yours and 'Clarke' on mine. As I remember, it stung like a bee sting. We joked that if we ever died skinny dipping, the authorities could use them to tell us apart. I never thought I would have to use it to prove who I am to my own brother." He held his right foot out in the sunlight. Albeit faded, Dane immediately recognized the tattoo.

"I don't understand," he said, looking at the old man he now realized may very well be his twin brother. "What's happened to you? If you're my brother, you're a forty five year old man, not a senior citizen. You haven't got progeria or some other rare aging disease do you?"

"Come inside and I'll explain." Clarke motioned for Dane to go inside. "Watch your step, it's hard to see coming in from the sunlight." Dane entered and paused a moment to let his eyes adjust. As he started down a long flight of steps, he could hear the door shut behind him, snuffing out the last of the outside light. Industrial lamp fixtures cast a dim light in the narrow stairwell. He guessed they were about twenty feet below ground when the stairs ended in a small vestibule. A set of doors were on the right. Clarke moved by him and pushed through into a second vestibule. Dane followed. There were doors on either side. Clarke pointed toward the doors on the right and Dane entered to find another set of stairs. They ended at yet another set of doors. A keypad on the wall blinked red. Clarke entered a series of numbers and the lock clicked open.

They entered a circular room about 40 feet in diameter stuffed with old furniture and antiques. Off to one side was a small area with recliner, bed, and kitchenette. "Home sweet home," said Clarke. The space reminded Dane of the eclectic antique stores and flea markets down in the historic district but with an efficiency apartment thrown in. "What is this place? You're not a hoarder are you?"

"First floor of an Atlas F missile launch control center, answered Clarke. "And no, I am not a hoarder. Just some things I picked up on my travels so to speak. There is another floor below this. That is where my workshop and all my equipment are located. It's completely surrounded by metal. Practically speaking, it's designed to withstand almost anything, including earthquakes. When it was built, it was believed even if a nuclear bomb struck nearby, it would be unaffected. It was also designed to protect against magnetic pulse, which makes it particularly useful for my purposes. On the other side," he said, pointing toward the door, "is the missile silo. It sits underneath the hill you saw behind the entrance. Best of all, it's far away from prying eyes."

"Geez, Clarke, you could've collected antiques in Santa Barbara. You didn't have to quit your job and become a recluse. But that's not what concerns me most. You haven't answered my question. What's happened to you? You look like an eighty year old man."

"I need to sit a while," Clarke said. He walked to the other side of the room and sat down in the old green recliner. "I'm sorry, only have one comfy chair, never planned to entertain." He pointed toward a table and chair a few feet away. Sit over there or bring it up closer if you like."

Dane pulled the chair close to Clarke. "OK, if you are finished rearranging the furniture, I am still waiting for your answer. Do I have to repeat my question?"

"Time," said Clarke.

"Don't jerk me around. Cut the crap Clarke, I know time makes everyone grow old, but that doesn't explain what I see happening with you. I need a straight answer from you or I'm leaving. I've already had a long day and I'm in no mood for this."

"Time Travel."

"Clarke, you know how this sounds. You need help…"

"Wait," Clarke interrupted, "before you jump to conclusions. I tell you I am a time traveler. Now, hear me out." He looked Dane in the eye. Satisfied his brother was paying attention, he continued, "While working at Avant Technologies, I got interested in the physics of time travel. I began my own sidebar research. Constrained by corporate bureaucracy, I decided to strike out on my own. To say the least, Avant Technologies was less than amicable at my departure and brought the full force of their legal Visigoths down on my head to prevent me from doing any private research. They pointed to some fine print provision on intellectual property in the employment contract I had signed. I knew they'd dog me till my dying day, so when they offered to release my 401k and sweeten it up with a generous payout for a lifetime no compete/no research agreement, I jumped on it. Of course I had other plans, so I took that and my savings and dropped off the grid to pursue my own research. After looking around for the right spot, I found this place and have been here ever since. That is, except when I rewind."

"Rewind?" asked Dane.

"That's what I call travelling to the past."

"Clarke, you know time travel isn't possible."

"Oh, not only is it possible, but it is also a given fact that everyone who ever existed has time traveled. Why you and I have been time traveling together since you arrived. Creeping ever forward in time."

"Well of course everyone travels forward in time. It's this rewinding as you call it that isn't possible."

"How do you know it's not possible?"

"The laws of physics say it's not."

"Well, at one time, the laws of physics said the world was flat and resided at the center of the universe. That's pretty much been debunked. I suppose I could take the next week explaining to you the first ten years of my research in worm holes and cosmic strings. Then I could take another day or two to review the construction of my time rewinder. But the truth is, Dane, my dear brother, you degreed in fine arts."

"Is that a cheap shot?"

"No offense intended. A fine arts degree is indeed a fine and noble accomplishment and a true benefit to society. But it's not theoretical physics."

"Agreed. So where does that leave us?"

"I think a practical demonstration would be the only method sufficient enough to convince you rewinding is possible."

"What do you mean?"

"I mean, I propose to rewind you."

"For the sake of argument, even if I really thought you had discovered how to time travel, I wouldn't agree to do it."

"Why not, Dane? It's easier than getting your toe tattooed."

"Well, when I asked you what had happened to make you look so old, you said it was time travel."

"What you see is the cumulative effect of hundreds of rewinds. I have come to believe that rewinding somehow causes the traveler to age prematurely. I think it has to do with how far back the rewind goes and how long it lasts. The first hundred or so times, I experienced no noticeable changes. But as I rewound more and more, the aging started and began to progress at an increasing rate with each rewind."

"And having said that, you would still want me to do this rewind thing?"

"How else can I convince you? As I said, I believe a single small rewind would have negligible, if any, effect."

"I still think this is a delusion. Sitting around in this bunker with all this old junk has driven you bonkers."

"Where do you think I got all this?" Clarke asked. "I picked up some souvenirs on my rewinds."

"This just gets better and better. You want me to believe you quit a great job and spent fifteen years living like a mole so you could go back in time and scavenge this junk? Clarke, this is nuts, totally nuts. I don't buy what you're trying to sell with this time travel phantasy of yours. I think you are sick, both physically and mentally. I believe we've got to get you some medical and psychological help right now, right this minute."

"Let me make you a proposition, Dane. You say you don't believe in time travel. If that's true, then nothing will happen when I try to rewind you. If that be the case, I'll do whatever you wish without argument or resistance. On the other hand, if you find you indeed were rewound, you will hear me out. What have you got to lose?"

"I'm gonna call your bluff. If I agree, what's involved?"

"I will be at the controls below. You will go outside to the top of the hill beside the entrance. There is a large stone in the ground. I have a big magnet buried underneath. Stand on the stone. You will feel a fleeting sensation similar to what you experience when a rollercoaster starts its downhill run. Everything will blur, then the next thing you see will be the past. It'll look like a misty morning on the bay, but that is normal. Well, normal for rewinding. I'll set the rewind for the moment just before you turned on the dirt path. You should be able to follow your approach until you park. I will then bring you back."

"Ha, wouldn't I have seen myself when I drove up? I remember looking up there and didn't see anyone, much less me."

"No, because you have not made that rewind yet," said Clarke. "You will remember it though after I bring you back."

"You're making my head smoke. So all I have to do is walk up to the top of the hill and stand there?"

"Yes."

"And then you'll come quietly?"

"If you aren't convinced, I'll comply with your wishes."

Dane thought about the proposition for a moment. "It's a deal."

"Alright, we'll rewind you after I rest a bit and we have some lunch."

* * *

After they ate, Clarke excused himself to go to his workshop in the lower level. He returned in a few minutes, holding a dog-eared book. "This is my journal. After my first few rewinds, I decided I needed a way to keep track of what I did and what happened as a result. I figured that if I did something while in rewind that altered the future, I should have a reference. So before each rewind, I would write down a few things or tuck a newspaper article inside to compare when I got back. That way I could tell if anything of significance changed. Then I could decide if it was good or bad. I could rewind to just before the previous rewind and stop myself if needed."

"If the future did change, wouldn't the journal change along with it?"

"While the rewind machine is active, it maintains its own sphere of time and space, unaffected by anything outside. During that time, in the sphere, everything stays constant. When the rewind machine is off, it marches along with the rest of the world, just like now."

"If you say so. I'm still not convinced."

"So let's convince you." Clarke set the journal on the table and opened it. Dane could see the pages crammed with small but legible handwriting. There were also numerous photographs and news clippings tucked in between the pages. Clarke flipped through the pages until he was almost at the back. "You said you remember looking up at the hill and not seeing anyone there, including yourself."

"Yeah."

Clarke handed Dane a ballpoint pen, then pointed to a blank line in the journal. "Before you go, record that then sign your name."

"Why?"

"Proof that you rewound."

"Now, I've got you," chortled Dane. He made a notation where Clarke had indicated, then followed him back up to the entry door.

"When you see yourself, wave," Clarke said, handing the journal to Dane.

"What's this for?"

"You keep it with you so you can't claim I altered it while you were rewinding. Just trust me on this one. Wave, and don't lose the journal."

"OK."

"So, go stand on the rock and wait. That's right above the old missile silo. It'll take me a few minutes to get down to my equipment and dial everything in."

It took a couple of minutes for Dane to exit and climb to the top of the hill. He found a large flat stone just where Clarke had said it would be. He reached his right toe out and gently tapped it, not knowing what to expect. It felt normal, so he planted both feet on its surface and turned to look back down the hill toward the entrance. He wondered if he was a fool to go along with Clarke's antics. Most likely, Clarke had locked the damn door behind him and was sitting in his madman's laboratory laughing until his brother gave up and went home. His thoughts were interrupted by a feeling that the stone had dropped out from underneath his feet. Instinctively, he looked down, relieved to see the stone still attached to his feet. Lifting his head, everything got blurry. He wondered if Clarke had put something in his food. Almost immediately it all came back into focus. The surroundings looked like a misty morning just as Clarke said it would. Dane glanced down toward the entrance. The van was there, but his rental was nowhere to be seen. He looked toward the spot where the path came in from the highway. His dark blue rental appeared, silhouetted against the horizon for an instant before it rolled through the solar panels. It whipped up a trail of dust. He watched until it came to a stop by the van and was immediately engulfed by the dust it had sucked along behind. Once it settled, Dane could see himself getting out and looking up.

Dane waved. Just as the other Dane waved back, he felt the falling away sensation again and everything got blurry. In an instant it cleared, the mist replaced by the bright Nebraska afternoon sun. Seeing his rental car parked by the van, he

185

wondered if he had really gone back in time or if Clarke had drugged him? He ran down the hill and jabbed at the intercom button until he heard the click of the door latch. He jerked the door open, causing Clarke to stumble forward into the sunlight. He grabbed Clarke's arm to steady him. "Clarke! Tell me what really happened. You slipped me some hallucinogenic drug or something. I know, I know, I bet it was a holographic projection. You used hidden cameras to video me driving up, then projected them in that mist stuff. Pretty slick."

"Do you remember?"

"Sure, I remember. It just happened. Why?"

"Did you see yourself?"

"Yeah."

"Did you wave?"

"Sure, just like you told me to. And the other me waved back."

"Fine, let's go inside." Clarke walked back in and started down the stairs. "Don't forget to close the door."

Dane was still clutching the journal as Clarke plopped down into his recliner. "I see you managed to hang onto the Journal."

"Sure, wouldn't want to lose your precious journal," Dane said, handing it to Clarke, who opened it to the last page of entries and held it up for Dane to see.

"What does it say?"

"What do you mean?"

"What did you write in the journal before you rewound?"

Dane saw his handwriting. He remembered, heart pounding; muscles tensing as his adrenal glands cranked into overdrive. There it was, in his own hand, written no more than fifteen minutes earlier.

'When I got here I parked next to the white van. I got out and looked around but didn't see anyone. – Dane Hartdegen'

Dane stood in silence, waiting for the rush of adrenaline to dissipate. "But I remember seeing someone on the top of the hill."

"No hallucinogenic drugs, no hidden cameras or holograms," Clarke said. "You went back. Waved at yourself. You changed your past and now it's a memory. But you also remember what you wrote in the journal."

"I gotta sit down," Dane said, dropping onto the other chair. "So it's true."

"Yes, it's true."

"Why did you wait all this time to tell me?"

"I should think one look at me and it would be obvious that I don't have much time. It's been some time since I last rewound. However, I continue to age at an accelerating rate."

"Damn Clarke, once you knew what was happening, why didn't you stop going back?"

"Couldn't stop till I got things right."

"What do you mean, got things right? Finish out your collection of antiques? Clarke, you could have done something to make this world a better place. Look at all the trouble in the Middle East. And what about racial strife right here in the good ol' USA? Kids starving in Africa. Couldn't you have done something about that?"

"You don't think I tried?" huffed Clarke. "Sure, I set out to change things. Thought it would be a cinch to make the world a better place. It just ain't that easy. No, you can't just snap your fingers and have all the pieces fall into place. Lorenz theorized

187

small changes to initial conditions that have the ability to affect later outcomes can result in large and often unanticipated differences in those outcomes on down the line. I was stupid enough to think if the final outcome was bad enough, any change would insure a better outcome."

"Sounds plausible to me."

"It took me maybe fifty rewinds just to figure out the basics before I tried anything big. Started out rewinding just a few minutes. Stayed on top of the hill. Wanted to make sure if the unwinding didn't work, I could just unlock the entrance door and start over. After I was convinced I could rewind as far in the past as I wanted, I experimented with leaving the hill and returning successfully. I designed a remote control to allow me to operate the rewind machine from the launch point at the top of the hill. Then I tried bringing things back with me. Once I was convinced it all worked, I began rewinding in earnest."

"What happened? Are you telling me this screwed up world is the best you could come up with?"

"No not at all, I'm trying to tell you the larger the outcome you try to improve by changing something in the past, the greater chance it will turn out worse. I know this from experience."

"What do you mean?"

"I know this is going to sound like the plot from some silly Sci-Fi movie but bear with me. Everything I am going to tell you is the truth. I assassinated Hitler before he came to power."

"It does sound silly. More than that it sounds like you are delusional. Couldn't you think of something a little less grandiose?"

"Chalk it up to being relatively young and a theoretical physicist. But the fact of the matter is that I did it."

"Sorry to tell you this Clarke, but the History Channel disagrees with you. Any day of the week, you can watch archival footage of Hitler and his henchmen slaughtering the Jews."

Clarke took a deep breath. "After rewinding, It took me six months to make my way from this hilltop to Germany and back again. I went to Munich in November of 1923 for the Beer Hall Putsch. History had recorded during the coup attempt Hitler was wounded and later captured. While in prison he wrote *Mein Kampf*, which paved the way for his rise to power. I shot him to death, secure in the thought that I had prevented World War II.

"When I unwound, I was horrified. Himmler had seized control of the Nazi Party, proving to be as ruthless a murderer as Hitler ever was. Unlike Hitler, he pursued the development of German nuclear capability. The Luftwaffe dropped the first atomic bomb on London at 7:00 pm on June 12, 1940. At 10:00 am the same day, Japan dropped an atomic bomb on Pearl Harbor. Both Great Britain and The United States surrendered. It's all there in a history book I bought before I went back and fixed things. It's over there," he said, pointing to a large bookcase, "if you want to read all that happened after that. I must warn you it's pretty shocking."

"So, you went back and fixed things?"

"Yes."

"How?"

"Much the same way I convinced you. I rewound to a time just before my 'assassinate Hitler' rewind. I waited outside the rewind sphere and stopped myself from going to Munich."

"And that was that. You fixed it simply by keeping yourself from going to Munich?"

"You don't speak German or Japanese do you?"

"Why try something so grandiose?" asked Dane.

"Chalk it up to being young, or at least younger than I am now, and foolish," sighed Clarke.

"You got it. Was that the only time you tried something like that?"

"No, like a fool, I thought it was a fluke. I tried going back to change the outcome of history again and again, always ending up making things worse each time. Then, I would have to go back and fix it. After I noticed the aging thing, I didn't want to risk making another change that turned out bad and dying before I could go back and fix it."

"That's a shame you had to give up," said Dane. "I can't help think of what things might be like if you had succeeded just one time."

"Didn't say I gave up. I just said I wasn't gonna rewind and try to change a major historical event." Clarke took a labored breath. "Pretty soon, you are going to hear a rumble and feel something like a little earthquake. Don't worry."

"Don't worry about what?"

"I've concluded that the rewind machine is too dangerous to leave behind. God forbid the government ever got ahold of it, or even worse, Facebook. I'm going to destroy it and all the information that goes along with it."

"Don't Clarke! Let me try. I'll be careful. I'll make sure good things happen; I promise," Dane begged.

"That I am depending on," Clark said, reaching to the side of his recliner and retrieving a large envelope. He undid the clasp and pulled out a handful of papers. He held them out to Dane. "Take these."

As Dane stood up he heard a rumble and felt the floor shake beneath his feet. "No, No," he winced. "You didn't have to do that. There had to be another way." Clarke gestured for Dane to take the papers. "What are those?" asked Dane.

"Another way."

"I don't understand."

"Take 'em," Clarke rasped, "I don't have enough strength to hold them out any longer." Dane took the papers. Clarke continued, "On my last rewind I went back to 1964. I invested $80,000 in Berkshire Hathaway stock. I set it up in a charitable trust. Today it is worth in the neighborhood of $1 billion. These are the documents appointing you trust manager. You will also find my last will and testament, naming you the sole beneficiary of my estate. I also made a few investments for myself along the way and you should be well situated."

"But Clarke…"

"But nothing," Clarke interrupted. "I finally figured it out. I couldn't make things better by changing the past, but I could make things better by changing the future. Unfortunately, I realized it too late. Dane, you are going to have to do it for me. You are going to take this money and make things better. Maybe not for the whole world, but for as many people as you can. Will you do that for me? I'm too tired, too old to go on."

"It's an awfully big responsibility, I don't know if I am up to it."

"Hell, it ought to be a walk in the park for someone who has traveled back it time. Now all you have to do is go in the other direction and do the right thing, but without the aid of a time machine. Take care." Clarke smiled, then fell silent.

A VITRUVIAN MAN[22]

Phillip Dietz's first rule of invisibility was to be still. His next was to find a good hiding place. Invisibility insulated, providing protection from the discomfort human interactions bring. He thought he had accomplished both when he selected a small table with a single chair, tucked snugly against the wall, between two larger tables already populated with fellow convention attendees. Having found the perfect location to see but not be seen, he sat down, feeling the warmth of the day's sun radiating from the red brick. A quick adjustment of his chair allowed a clear view of the human bustle along the sidewalk. His own small town boasted no such outdoor cafés and he relished the opportunity to sit in the open air listening to the steady urban hum and watching the ebb and flow of people along the street. In fact, listening and watching were his favorite things to do. Whether at work, church or a party, he would find a strategic spot to conduct his observations and search out alignments. He felt safe in this vicarious participation in the social process - no worries about saying the wrong thing or wearing the wrong clothes, able to pass judgment without being judged. No need to guess about what he should feel, no angst over his emotional ambivalence. No feelings equaled no discomfort.

The smell of coffee and fresh bread floated over the tables, occasionally interrupted as a waiter whisked by dragging the odor of Chablis and pot stickers along behind. Phillip sat back, iced tea in hand, drinking in the tableau before him.

---

[22] "A Vitruvian Man" is a revision of an Amazon Kindle Edition under the title "The Vitruvian Man", 2/15/2015.

To one side, a mixed group chatted, sipping cheap house wine, and casually checking smart phones. On the other, a group of young men, collars open, noisily drinking draft beer and wolfing down Buffalo wings. They were engulfed in a raucous discussion.

"Come on, you know as well as I do the government is hiding something out in the Nevada desert," sweater vest said, pointing to plaid shirt.

"Yeah," added black glasses, "and don't forget the Philadelphia Experiment."

"Isn't that where they wrapped some ship with about a zillion feet of telephone wire and hooked it to a battery to make it disappear?" asked blue shirt and khakis.

Phillip adjusted his gaze, bringing sweater vest in alignment with a World Examiner newspaper dispenser sporting the garish headline: JFK Alive! - and behind that, a cab with an advertisement for Ancient Aliens on the History Channel. Phillip had honed his skills through hours of patient observation to the point he recognized alignments everywhere.

He continued his listening. Others would have called this eavesdropping, but he relied on it. He resisted the notion that it was shallow, naïve, and sometimes uncompassionate. Lots to be learned from observation. He considered it the ultimate way to keep up without the awkwardness of actually talking with anyone. He learned all he wanted through the simple act of watching and listening without the risks of social intercourse or the complications of emotional engagement. No need for laborious conversation, for in a split second, he assessed appearance, mannerisms, features, and companions, then passed judgment. Through the most casual observation or slimmest snippet of conversation, he categorized upbringing, occupation, attitudes, personality and character.

The other table enjoyed its own busy conversation.

"Here is a photo of the ultrasound," long brown hair said passing her phone to button-down collar. "It's in 3D."

"Very nice," he said passing it along. "Just what am I looking at, if you don't mind?"

"Don't be silly," piped in hoop earrings, "It's the baby. There are the fingers, there are the toes, and," she chortled pointing to the center of the tiny screen, "there's his hose."

Brown hair giggled and covered her face.

"Have you felt him move yet?" asked purple eye shadow and margarita.

"No, but my doctor says it can be anytime now."

Shifting his head slightly, Phillip found he could line up brown hair with the Blessed Mother Catholic Church diagonally across the street and a billboard for Snuggies baby diapers on the freeway beyond. Sometimes these patterns lasted but a moment, other times, they lingered as long as he cared to look.

Phillip checked back on sweater vest's alignment only to see it dissolve as the Ancient Aliens cab pulled away. Soon, brown hair and her companions would leave and her alignment with the church and billboard would end. No matter, there would be other alignments to uncover, there always were.

Phillip sipped his tea in the afternoon sun, absorbed in the patterns and alignments of the café patrons, sidewalk pedestrians, and the traffic all around him. He had no questions to answer, no social games to play. He just observed.

The patterns of the city reminded him of the flocks of migrating birds he often watched as a child; swirling, undulating, sometimes almost invisible, then suddenly thick and black against the sky. He watched the traffic move along the busy street. The café occupied one corner of an intersection with a small roundabout at its heart. Cars, trucks, motorcycles, and bicycles whirled around like a carnival ride. Instead of the brass ring, they searched for the fleeting path to their final destination. Looking straight ahead between the two tables, Phillip could see a stone obelisk, jutting skyward from the central island. It gleamed yellow in the afternoon sun,. The traffic flowed on without stopping as a bus slipped through to the curb. Passengers stepped off and squeezed through the waiting boarders before dissolving into the flow of pedestrians.

As the afternoon passed, the sun drifted down to the tops of the buildings, casting long shadows across the sidewalks and streets. For Phillip, the constant movement and hum of the city served as a dreamy lullaby. His eyes grew heavy. He missed his normal routine. He found travelling stressful and happily felt his tension begin to drain away. After the long day, he wanted to trudge back to his room and fall into his bed for a much deserved nap.

He looked around to signal the waiter for his bill. As his eyes swept back and forth, the obelisk, which glowed all the brighter as the shadows crawled across the street toward the island, drew his attention. It stood serene and silent against the backdrop of constant motion and sound of the city. A sudden movement caused Phillip to sit upright in his seat. He gasped as a man suddenly sprang from the base of the obelisk. No unseen door had opened. No portal had materialized. The stone surface of the obelisk remained smooth and unblemished. Yet, a man had appeared in full view just as if he stepped out from a dark doorway into the sunlight. Phillip, the man, and the obelisk were in perfect alignment, so much so the figure was perfectly framed against the glowing amber stone.

Moving in a straight line toward Phillip, the man's wavy hair bounced wildly about his head. His skin, drawn tight over his naked body, glowed like burnished bronze in the afternoon sun. Philip, reminded of da Vinci's iconic Vitruvian Man, mentally drew a circle around the figure framed against the square base of the obelisk. In a few strides, he had reached the edge of the island, leaping into the street without disrupting the frantic flow of cars and cabs. He raced up on the sidewalk and through the crowd of people waiting to cross without as much as a brush of a shoulder. All the while, the man kept his gaze firmly on Phillip who now abandoned his usual nonchalant pose and leaned straight forward in his chair. Like a schoolboy caught peeping into the girl's locker room, Phillip was unnerved and a queasy lump formed in his chest.

The man glided between the crowded café tables. Philip was sure heads would turn; conversations would stop. At home, everything would have ground to a halt at the spectacle of a man running naked through the Square. Apparently, that was not the case in the big city. Black glasses continued his discussion, now focused on the Roswell incident. None of the patrons seemed to notice. From the moment he had appeared, the man had moved in a straight line, now so close, Phillip could only see the tip of the obelisk above his head. Now, only the two tables remained separating them. With eyes firmly fixed on Phillip, he reached forward as if to touch brown hair's shoulder. A reddish brown smear covered the palm of his hand.

"Oh my God," she gasped, reaching down and cupping her belly with her hands. "I just felt him move."

Then, everything stopped. It was as if someone had hit the pause button. The sea of motion and sound that had flowed around him just a moment before hung frozen in a panoramic still life. Black glasses leaned forward in his chair, mouth open and forefinger shoved in the face of a wide-eyed red hair and freckles. A teenager floated above the sidewalk, caught in midair as she jumped from the door of a bus. Purple eye shadow sipped endlessly from her margarita.

The silence was complete. Phillip had not heard such silence since he took a school trip to Mammoth Cave years before. The guide waited until they had traveled deep inside the cave to turn out the lights and ask the school children to remain absolutely silent. Then as now, Phillip could only hear his faint heartbeat thrum within his eardrums.

As soon as Phillip realized he was moving his eyes, he found he could also move his head. He then tested his arm by gingerly setting down the glass of tea he had been holding motionless about an inch above the table top. None-the-less, he could not detect any movement other than his own.

"Are you coming?" a voice erupted in his head, startling Phillip. "We must go," came the voice again.

Phillip searched frantically for the source, focusing at last on the uncompromising face and single set of eyes returning his gaze.

"Yes," the voice affirmed, as the man gestured to Phillip with an open hand.

The first rule to remain invisible is to be still. All else remained frozen. Though he was sure that he hadn't said a word, a queasy knot tightened in Phillip's chest. Adrenaline amplified each pounding heartbeat in his ears. Why had he moved, giving himself away? As a child, when he awoke in the deep of night, he would lie motionless in his bed so what lurked in the dark could not find him. No movement to draw attention. Be still and the man will go away.

"Come," the voice commanded.

"No," Phillip heard himself blurt out, violating another rule – don't engage. Although he was certain he hadn't actually said anything, he opened his mouth to see if it was true.

"No need for that, you need only think and I will hear."

Phillip clamped his mouth shut. Never-the-less, as soon as he thought he didn't believe, he heard his voice implore, "Leave me alone."

"It is not your choice."

"I won't go!"

"Come," the voice commanded again.

To his utter dismay, Phillip found himself slowly standing up. As much as he tried, he could not resist the outstretched hand before him. Slowly, stiffly, Phillip moved forward.

As their fingertips touched, his surroundings whirled past in a confused snarl of colors and shapes. Phillip found himself running step for step with the man across a shabby, vacant street. He did not recognize the narrow canyon of grey buildings. He saw a clear path aligned in a diagonal from the corner of the intersection ahead to the corner of the next intersection and then straight to a small church. They continued on, bounding from sidewalk to street and back again without breaking stride. He wanted desperately to stop, but like a car careening out of control on black ice, he continued inextricably running forward. They traversed the expanse of crumbling asphalt in a heartbeat, leaping once again onto the sidewalk. He calculated their path as they jumped back into the side street heading straight for the weather-beaten church and realized if they didn't stop, they would run

199

headlong into the moss-covered bricks about 5 feet to the right of the door.

The steady thump, thump of his footsteps echoed the pounding of his heart. Just as they reached the wall, he sensed the man's eyes were on him. Everything stopped as the impulse to turn his head entered his mind. Phillip was in mid-stride. He was so close to the wall he could see the grains of sand in the crumbling mortar between the bricks. A tiny spider dangled motionless at the end of a grey thread suspended from the window ledge above.

Everything had moved so fast Phillip had little time to question what was happening. Now, his mind flooded as his thoughts, left back at the café, finally caught up. With them came an immense feeling of fear. His life, so carefully constricted, seemed tumbling out of control. "I don't want to be here. Take me back."

"Your path is ahead," said the voice.

"I don't want a path. I didn't ask for a path. Whatever this is, I don't want it." Dread whelmed up inside Phillip. He desperately wanted to turn away from the wall looming inches from his face, but he remained motionless.

"All will be known to you soon," the voice said inside his head. "We cannot linger here, ours is a continuing journey from which there is no respite. As for this moment, we are like the traveler whose thoughts wander to far off places while he walks, losing all sense of place until he finds himself well down the path with no recollection of his journey."

The man reached forward to the wall with his right hand as his left lightly touched Phillip's arm. Before the church melted away, he watched the man's bronze fingertips slide smoothly into the brick.

They emerged, running through a wooded area. Although he had never been in those woods before, Phillip knew they were headed straight for an ancient Indian mound hidden deep inside. His mind floated above the trees. A panorama stretched from horizon to horizon. He recognized the outcroppings of rocks, the streams and ancient paths, trod thousands of years ago, that marked the way. This island of green laid at the edge of the grey city.

"You will begin to see," said the man's voice.

"See what?"

The mound loomed into view as they reached the crest of a low ridge. The grass-covered cone grew out of the Midwestern plain reminiscent of the pyramids rising out of the Egyptian desert. As they approached, the faint murmur of laughter and tears mixed with the songs and prayers of long forgotten tongues, drifting by like the last of a morning mist. Phillip did not understand the words, but knew they represented the hopes and fears of those who had passed before.

A figure, clothed in a mottled green robe, stood at the top of the mound. As they approached, the man once again touched Phillip's arm lightly. They stood motionless before the figure whose face was hidden. No matter how hard Phillip tried, he could not pierce the shadowy depths of the hood.

Phillip felt unnerved as a presence foraged the inner reaches of his soul. From his vantage point, Phillip could see alignments and patterns stretching out to the horizon in an intricate pattern like the spidery sinews in a dream catcher. Their course was marked in many ways: a stone outcropping, a spring or church steeple. He recognized the marks as easily as finding the faces of old friends in a crowd.

He had no sense of how much time had passed since they left the café. It could have been a minute as well as month. He imagined flying high above, his mind drinking in the alignments and patterns that lay beneath him in an ever-expanding bargello.

"The Steward is finished; our path lies before us" said the man's voice in his head pulling him back to himself.

"What's happening to me?"

"You have spent your life standing on the periphery, observing, hiding from that which elevates man above all other animals. Now, you will begin to gather.

"I don't understand."

"You must experience before you can understand."

"Please I don't want to understand anything – I don't need to experience anything. I just want to go back. Just let me go and I'll get back on my own."

The Steward pointed toward the horizon. As near as Phillip could determine, they had traveled a straight line from the moment the man had touched his hand in the café until they reached this spot. Now, the robed figure directed them in a different direction. All that had happened flooded back into Phillip's consciousness. He shuddered, chest knotting again, harsh bile driven by fear coursing through his body. He wanted to escape, bolt headlong away from the man and the Steward, but terror stiffened his muscles. His heart pounded dully in his ears and he felt as if his blood had congealed in his veins.

The instant the man drew his arm away, the mound and the Steward vanished. As they ran straight forward in a steady rhythm, the terror that had seized Phillip subsided. Their path unfurled before them through places unfamiliar to Phillip, but always evident, shimmering off into the distance. It was marked along the way with a variety of talismans each as familiar to

Phillip as his own front door. At each of these, additional paths intersected, streaming on to the horizon in their own tremulous glow.

Phillip peered in wonder at the gleaming interlace of paths.

"They are the ley lines," offered the man. "Alignments that traverse the earth providing a framework linking significant sites of natural and spiritual importance. The ancients knew and revered these powerful alignments. Through the millennia, they have been called by many names. For instance, the Chinese called them the 'Dragon Currents'. To the Incas, they were the 'Ceques' or 'Spirit Lines.' For the Aborigines, they formed the 'Turingas' or 'Dream Lines'. The alignments and the structures at their intersections focus spiritual and earth energies which can be tapped. They were vitally important to the existence of ancient man. These energies were critically linked to all aspects of their lives from their spiritual belief systems to their agricultural practices. Modern man no longer thinks he needs them."

"That's absurd! Ancient myths are just that – myths!" Phillip protested

"Do you find the presence of the Earth's magnetic fields absurd? Do you scoff at cell phone signals bouncing all about? You accept gravity as an absolute certainty exerting an invisible force on everything in the universe. If you accept those as real, why then reject the notion that ley lines are the result of natural and spiritual energies?"

Phillip fell back into contemplation as they ran toward the ever retreating horizon. The rolling countryside was occasionally interrupted by a farm, village or small town. They never strayed from the straight line in which they ran, passing through any and all things in their path, including the people, undetected and undeterred.

At first, with his usual detached interest, Phillip merely observed. However, as he continued, he began to feel something which made him intensely uncomfortable. Gradually, he began to realize he was sensing the peoples' emotions both individually and collectively. Initially, he experienced them like the subtle shift of an autumn wind from cool to crisp. Their intensity grew, becoming more invasive, lingering in his soul. Horrified, he tried to resist. He had spent his life building walls, sheltering himself from the distress of emotion.

As his capacity to experience and absorb their feelings of joy, sorrow, fear, hate, and love grew, his ability to focus on the veneer of physical appearance, melted away. He carried their feelings with him no matter how far he ran. Each encounter added more. Eventually, he could sense the waiting emotions long before he could see any people. Like a child ill from eating too many sweets, he was nauseated by the emotions he carried, roiling inside.

On they ran, never stopping, never veering from their path. Phillip began to strain under the fatigue. He had not felt the least bit taxed at the beginning. However, each emotion he absorbed added to his growing exhaustion. The rolling Midwestern landscape gave way to rocky foothills and eventually rugged mountains. Here, the desolation of poverty and drug-fed depression constantly assaulted him. He felt the suffocating choke of hopelessness dragging him down as they struggled to the crest of a steep ridge. The burden crushed his soul. He wanted desperately to rest, but his legs would not stop. All the while, the man ran silently alongside. Phillip lurched forward on stumbling legs. The emotions he carried thrashed about within his psyche like loose cargo in a ship caught in a maelstrom. Topping the ridge, he saw their path lead down to a Steward standing by a small spring gushing from a rocky outcrop.

Phillip staggered down the side of the ridge through the loose rock. Just as he thought he would run the Steward over; he felt the touch of his companion's hand on his arm. Everything stopped. They stood motionless before the Steward. Complete silence surrounded them. Sunlight cambered through the droplets of spring water hanging motionless above the glistening stones in the streambed. Even the air stood still. Phillip struggled to catch a glimpse of the Steward's face in the bright sunlight, but a shadow, black as night, filled the void. The presence combed the deepest fissures of Phillip's soul, gathering the emotions he had amassed. As it departed, he felt brief moment of stillness, as profound as the frozen landscape around him.

"The Steward is finished, our path lies before us," the man said, as the Steward motioned toward the horizon.

"What is happening to me?" Phillip asked. "I can't take any more of this. I barely made it here as it is."

"You have started gathering."

"Well, I don't want to gather, if it means going through that again." As the words formed in his mind, Phillip felt a twinge of emptiness inside as the man touched his arm.

The rugged granite peaks evaporated, replaced by sandy dunes. They ran straight forward in a steady rhythm until the green-grey ocean filled the horizon. Phillip filled his emptiness with the emotions of those they passed along the way. Unsated, his hunger gnawed at him as they crossed the ocean's empty expanse. He welcomed the sight of bluffs rising from the sea. They sped across the rocky coastline to the sheer wall of the cliffs towering above. The man took Phillip's arm as they passed through the rough exterior of stone as easily as walking through the rain. They continued unimpeded through solid rock, like walking through a wheat field on a sunny day. Their path rose gradually until they emerged on the surface, high above the sea, moving cross country once again.

He continued to draw in emotions as they passed through numerous villages and hamlets. Although he was still uncomfortable with the idea of gathering, the emptiness soon receded replaced by a fullness he had not anticipated. They entered a region of rivers lined with steep limestone cliffs. Small villages lay tucked in shallow valleys. Once again, Phillip strained under the burden of the emotions he carried. He wanted to rest, but he was compelled on by a force he could not comprehend or resist. Their path led to a cave tucked into a rocky escarpment. Phillip struggled up the steep embankment, reaching the opening just as he felt his whole body would burst apart. He knew a Steward waited within.

They plunged headlong into blackness until they reached a large gallery bathed in the glow of firelight. The Steward stood at its center. The smooth cavern walls were covered with ancient paintings depicting a pantheon of hunt and predatory animals. Their images danced in the flickering light. Thirty thousand years prior, the artist had signed his masterpiece in the form of a single red ochre handprint. The man stopped in front of the paintings. He gazed intently at each figure, studying each stroke. He touched his right hand to the palm print on the wall. It was a perfect fit.

The Man turned and faced the Steward. Phillip followed suit and opened his soul. The glut of emotions he carried, drained away. The weight of his burden now lifted, leaving him with a gnawing emptiness. The gallery dissolved as the Steward motioned to the black recesses of the cave.

They burst into bright sunlight. Verdant lowlands rolled out ahead. They ran on until they reached the warm, blue ocean. Their path stretched out over the vast sea to a blazing desert wasteland beyond.

The emotions Phillip gathered from the few nomadic bands roaming the barren landscape did little to satisfy the hunger in his soul. Even under the sun's harsh glare, their path shone clear and straight through the featureless desert.

"How long have you followed these paths?" Phillip asked.

"Since the day I placed my mark in that cave."

"Are there others?"

"Yes, now and before."

"Before?"

"Mankind has followed these paths since the first mother felt joy at the movement of her unborn child."

"Are the others like us?"

"'A time to plant, and a time to pluck up that which is planted' Ecclesiastes 3. We Gatherers reap up feelings of hate, love, sorrow, joy, and the like as we move along our paths. When we are filled and can no longer gather more, we give them to the Stewards. They in turn transfer these feelings to the Sowers, who plant them among humankind."

"You quote the bible?" Phillip asked

"Knowledge may also be gained along our path. Is that what you want to know?"

"I want to know why."

"You once thought I resembled The Vitruvian Man – an interesting observation. The Roman architect Vitruvius saw man as the greatest work. It was his idea that man could be made to fit inside a circle and a square. The proportions defined by Vitruvius were later employed by da Vinci to illustrate his famous drawing.

This was not a simple exercise in geometry. The notion holds deep significance. Philosophers have long held that the circle represents the spiritual or cosmic, while the square, the secular and earthly. Combined, the circle and square represent the world in its entirety, the union of spiritual and temporal. Placing man in both is a philosophical statement that envisions him as a microcosm of the world itself. The union of the spiritual and the temporal is man's defining attribute, differentiating him from the common beast. In Man, that union is experienced and expressed though emotions.

"What makes a young woman leave the comforts of her home and travel halfway around the world to deliver food and medicine to those suffering here in the desert? What makes an infant suddenly laugh? I tell you, it is the emotional bond linking all humankind one to another. It is our task, Gathers, Sowers and Stewards, to spread that throughout the world."

"But all this is too much for me," rasped Phillip. "The sorrow, the hurt, the hate, that burden is too great."

"Do you not also know joy, pleasure and love?"

"Yes, I do, and it is indeed wonderful."

"To accept one is to accept the other. To understand one is to understand the other. We are not human – not complete - one without the other."

The concentration of refugees, frail and terrified, wandering through the barren wasteland increased. No longer resistant, Phillip drank in the agony of their famine. Gaunt mothers carried listless infants, stomachs distended, too weak even to cry. Sharp talons of fear and desolation clawed holes in Phillip's soul, desperately seeking entrance. He reeled under the burden. His pain seared unbearably. The unrelenting sun did not scorch his skin and parch his throat as it would an ordinary man.

It was his soul - erupting like a blast furnace gone berserk. He lurched forward. Ahead, women drew water from an ancient well, oblivious of the Steward standing in their midst.

Phillip struggled painfully forward until he stood face to face with the Steward. She reached up and pulled the hood from her face. For the first time, he could see her features clearly. In her grim eyes, he could see every face for every emotion that flowed out of his soul. The faces drifted into the recesses of the Steward's eyes. Once they had all passed, they were replaced with the frozen images of the refugees around the well. He was at once sad and relieved to feel his burden drain away.

The Steward pulled her hood up, covering her face. She raised her arm and pointed to a shimmering path rising up from the barren desert floor. Phillip, finally ready to fill his emptiness, anxiously turned to look at the man who had been his constant companion. He saw an old, bent figure. Phillip's tattered clothes flapped loosely on the man's frail body as he hobbled forward. Drawing close, the old man reached out with pale, bony fingers and touched the bronzed skin of Phillip's chest. He began to whisper.

The desert melted away and he found himself striding alone through lush jungle. He passed through villages whose inhabitants celebrated birth and mourned death, danced at harvest time, and sang songs to remember their ancestors. He drank in their emotions as he followed his shimmering pathway.

He knew somewhere in a bleak desert, someone was wearing his clothes, stripped from a pale, mummified corpse. In a small Midwestern town, a weekly newspaper carried a headline on the 3rd page reading 'Local Man Disappears While at Convention'. The old man's whispered words lingered in his ears.

"So my path ends and yours begins."

APPENDIX
INTRODUCTION TO INVERSION

Inversion - Not Your Ordinary Stories, is all about speculative fiction. From my viewpoint, this form of fiction places us in a world where the Laws, those regularly occurring or apparently inevitable phenomenon that govern what happens to us, operate differently than what we would expect. In the speculative fiction world, the rules as we know them do not always apply. Or could it be the rules as we thought we knew them?

Speculative fiction aims to explore our world as it would be altered by posing the question What if? The most appealing and freeing aspect of speculative fiction is that, like the worlds it creates, it is not bound by the traditional genres of Science Fiction, Fantasy, and Horror. In fact it is not bound by any genre. It is free to adventure anywhere it likes as long as anywhere is a creation of imagination and speculation.

Inversion means turning upside down or inside out, reversal of a normal order or relation. What better title for a collection of speculative fiction stories? When you ask What if?, the result is not your ordinary story.

Some of these stories have been previously published, either in print or online. They have been identified throughout. I wish to express my appreciation to those editors who were willing to publish my work and encourage the reader to visit these other publications.

I would also like to thank the members of the Danville Writers Group, who have read many preliminary drafts of these stories and offered their feedback and assistance.

Finally, I would like to thank Joan Stansbury, affectionately known as the Queen of Commas, for her editorial assistance.

ABOUT THE AUTHOR

Paul Stansbury is a lifelong native of Kentucky. Now retired, he lives in Danville, Kentucky. He is the owner of Sheppard Press. He is the author of *Inversion - Not Your Ordinary Stories, Inversion II - Creatures, Fairies, and Haints Oh My!, Inversion III - The Lighter Shades of Greys, Inversion IV – Another Infusion of Speculative Fiction,* and *Down By the Creek – Ripples and Reflections,* all published by Sheppard Press. His novelette, *Little Green Men?* was published by The Society of Misfit Stories.

His stories appearing in print/e-book anthologies:

- "A Game Of Tag" and "Dark Meat" appeared in Brief Grislys published by Apocryphile Press
- "Sigaforgas" appeared in Neo-Legends To Last A Deathtime published by KY Story
- "The Ghost Eye" appeared in Frightening published by SEZ Publishing
- "Takers" appeared in Out of the Cave published by MacKenzie Publishing
- "Phantasmal" appeared in In Media Res, Stories From the In- Between published by Writespace Houston
- "Under the Wolf Moon" appeared in Nocturnal Natures published by Zimbell House Publishing
- "Spirit Painter" appeared in Book 3: 30 Authors - 30 Stories published by Flash Fiction Magazine
- "Exiled" appeared in See Through My Eyes: A Ghost Mystery Anthology published by Fantasia Divinity Magazine
- "Selkie Cove" appeared in Mirrors & Thorns - An OWS Ink Dark Fairy Tale Anthology published by Catterfly Publishing (A Division of OWS Ink. LLC)
- "Little Green Men?" appeared in The Society of Misfit

Stories Presents...Volume One published by Bards and Sages Publishing

- "The Girl In The Harvest Moon" appeared in Autumn's Harvest: An Autumn Fantasy Anthology published by Fantasia Divinity Magazine
- "Mulded" appeared in Anthology Askew 006 published by Rhetoric Askew
- "The Scroll And The Silver Kazoo" appeared in The Rabbit Hole, Weird Tales Volume 1 published by The Writers Co-op
- "Word Of Mouth" appeared in THEMA Vol. 21, No. 2 Summer 2019 published by the THEMA Literary Society
- "Do You Know Why You Are Here Today?" appeared in Hallucination published by pacificREVIEW, a San Diego State University Press Journal 2019
- Do You Remember How To Fly?" appeared in Mad Scientist Journal Summer 2019.
- "Yovido, in the Ivaldi System", "The Usual Conclusion" and "The Red Star" appeared in Our Universes - a Boyle County Public Library Chapbook published through Sheppard Press, 2019.
- "Mangalo" appeared in The Weird and Whatnot November 16, 2019.
- "A Thanksgiving To Remember" and "I Can't Believe I Fell For This One", appeared in Memories Worth Remembering II - a Boyle County Public Library book published through Sheppard Press, 2020.
- "Ndoto Vumbi", appeared in Going-Off-The-Grid: Down in the Dirt - March 2020, Volume 169.
- "Unnoticed" appeared in The Rabbit Hole, Weird Tales Volume 0 published by The Writers Co-op, 2020.

- "Dark Harvest" appeared in Lifeboat - Down in the Dirt December 2021, v190 and Stardust in Hand (by assorted writers and artists from the September - December 2021 issues of Down in the Dirt Magazine), 2021.
- "Decisions", "Quest for the Phantom Firefly," and "The Green Gate", appeared in Memories Worth Remembering III - a Boyle County Public Library book published through Sheppard Press, 2022.
- "Decisions", "Quest for the Phantom Firefly," and "The Green Gate", appeared in *Memories Worth Remembering III* - a Boyle County Public Library book published through Sheppard Press, 2022.
- "Retirement", appeared in *Short Fiction Potpourri – A* Boyle County Public Library book published through Sheppard Press, 2022.

His work has also appeared in a variety of on-line publications. His poetry has appeared in The Rising Phoenix Review, Young Ravens Literary Review, Strange Poetry and Kentucky Monthly.

He is Scheduling Coordinator for The Jeanne Penn Lane Celebration of Kentucky Writers.

BOOKS FROM SHEPPARD PRESS

Down By The Creek – Ripples and Reflections
by Paul Stansbury
ISBN 978-0-9986516-0-6 paperback
ISBN 978-0-9986516-1-3 e-book

Inversion – Not Your Ordinary Stories
by Paul Stansbury
ISBN 978-0-9986516-3-7 paperback
ISBN 978-0-9986516-4-4 e-book

Inversion II – Creatures, Fairies, and Haints Oh My!
by Paul Stansbury
ISBN 978-0-9986516-5-1 paperback
ISBN 979-8-9870989-1-2 e-book

Inversion III – The Lighter Shades Of Greys
by Paul Stansbury
ISBN 978-0-9986516-7-5 paperback
ISBN 978-0-9986516-8-2 e-book

Inversion IV – Another Infusion of Speculative Fiction
by Paul Stansbury
ISBN 978-0-9986516-9-9 paperback
ISBN 979-8-9870989-0-5 e-book

By George – A Collection Of Childhood Experiences and Anecdotes
by George Herbert Stansbury, Jr.
ISBN 978-0-9986516-2-0 paperback

Migrant Times and Other Musings
by George Boursaw
Available only at Lulu - https://www.lulu.com

Memories Worth Remembering
by Various Authors
Available only at Lulu - https://www.lulu.com

Our Universes
by Various Authors
Available only at Lulu - https://www.lulu.com

Memories Worth Remembering II
by Various Authors
Available only at Lulu - https://www.lulu.com

Memories Worth Remembering III
by Various Authors
Available only at Lulu - https://www.lulu.com

Letters from Mabel - Sentiments From Sisters That Cross The Miles...
by Ruth Rogers
Available only at Lulu - https://www.lulu.com

Short Fiction Potpourri
by Various Authors
Available only at Lulu - https://www.lulu.com